KATE FOSTER 1/1

DYNNU ODDI AR STOC

WITHDRAWN FROM STOCK

© Copyright Rachel Amphlett 2014
The copyright of this book belongs to Rachel Amphlett
No reproduction without permission

The names, characters and events in this book are
used fictitiously. Any similarity to actual people
living or dead, events or locales is entirely
coincidental.

National Library of Australia Cataloguing-in-Publication entry:
Amphlett, Rachel – author

Before Nightfall

ISBN: 978-0-9922685-2-7 (paperback)
Amphlett, Rachel, author
Before Nightfall
658.4

Before Nightfall

Rachel Amphlett

Chapter 1

Northumberland, UK

Kate Foster's breath escaped her lips in short, shallow bursts.

The sack, which had been placed over her head when she had first been attacked, clung to her mouth and nose with each inhaled gasp.

Condensation prickled against her face, the lack of air suffocating. Her heart beat rapidly, hammering against her ribcage, while a trickle of sweat worked its way between her breasts.

The hard wooden chair pierced the denim fabric of her jeans, and she wriggled backwards, trying to ease the pressure on her pelvic bone.

'Stay still,' said a voice to her right. Her head twitched, and she held her breath, sensing the man as he drew closer. She caught a faint trace of his scent through the musty fabric of the sackcloth – sweat, a hint of hours-old aftershave.

Her heart skipped a beat, and her stomach clenched. The smell grew stronger, and she turned her head from side to side, trying to gauge the man's exact location. A faint echo of his shower gel lingered in the air between them, a mixture of musk and jasmine.

'No-one's coming to get you,' he murmured in her ear.

Kate jumped in her seat, not realising his proximity had been so close. Her heart raced harder, and she exhaled, trying to keep calm, the rushing sound in her ears now deafening.

A low chuckle vibrated next to her skin. She twisted, trying to gain some distance between them.

She'd lost all sense of time. This morning, she'd been talking to three colleagues outside, taking advantage of the rare sunshine that had bathed the courtyard.

The attack had been swift, well-coordinated, with no warning.

Her jewellery and watch had been removed from her, and then she'd been shoved into a small room with her colleagues, and told to stay silent.

Maybe an hour had passed, during which time her colleagues had been taken one by one from the room, leaving the remaining captives to their own thoughts.

Then, the hostage takers had returned for her, dragging her from the sitting position she'd been forced to adopt, the sack over her head damp with condensation from her breath.

She'd felt a hard surface under her feet, and then a door had slammed shut behind her. She'd been forced into a chair, before her wrists were pushed through plastic cuffs and secured.

Now, her breathing increased as she tried to remember what she'd been told, what to do to keep her captor calm. She worked her wrists, trying to loosen the cuffs and keep the circulation flowing through her fingers.

'They'll pay you,' she whispered, then coughed and cleared her throat before repeating herself. 'They'll pay you. To let me go. To keep me safe.'

An exasperated sigh escaped the man's lips.

Kate held her breath, and then jumped as the sackcloth was ripped off her head. She blinked in the rays of light shining through the grubby farmhouse window.

'No!'

The voice drew her attention back to the man who was now standing in front of her, hands on hips, glaring.

'Don't ever try to bargain with them,' he said, then turned and strode across the room to a table. He threw the sackcloth onto it and slumped into another chair, facing her, his foot tapping an unknown beat on the floor. 'You do that, they're going to feed on your desperation.'

Kate shifted in her seat and watched his heel bounce up and down, and then caught him staring at her. She blushed and lowered her gaze.

The hostage course was so damn hard – only three days to remember everything the instructors were trying to teach her, on top of a bad case of jetlag after her flight from the US two days ago. The difficulty rating went through the ceiling when the taller of the two, now berating her, looked so bloody good in the tight black t-shirt he was wearing with his jeans.

She raised her head and watched the man who was running his hand through his unkempt brown hair, frustration etched across his face.

He appeared to ignore her discomfort. '*Small steps.* Build up a rapport – don't discuss politics, religion or your own situation. Keep it simple. Ask for small favours.' His voice rose. 'And under *no* circumstances talk about paying a ransom. *Ever.*'

He rose from the chair and stalked towards her. 'That's the hostage negotiator's job, and you could ruin everything he's trying to do to save you. Remember the basics we discussed in the classroom yesterday?'

Kate swallowed. She found her concentration wavering as she stared into his green eyes, sure she could see gold flecks around the edge of his irises, and then cursed inwardly as her bottom lip quivered. Although it was a simulated kidnapping, it had been frighteningly real.

Her eyes stung, and she blinked, inhaled deeply and tried to ignore the heat in her face. 'Can you at least untie me?'

He waited for a heartbeat, and then turned, shaking his head. 'You sort her out,' he said over his shoulder and pushed his way through a door which led to the yard outside.

Kate's mouth dropped open in indignation, before her attention was drawn to another, older man approaching her.

He reached into the back pocket of his jeans, pulled out a knife and bent down. He flicked the blade open. As he raised the blade, he glanced up, his grey eyes twinkling with humour.

'Ignore Finn,' he said. 'He's having a bad day.'

A faint smile stole across Kate's face, and she sniffed. 'Really, Steve? What's he like on a good day?'

He smirked. 'You've got another day and a half to go, so I'll have a word, get him to play nice. Keep still.'

She nodded and watched as he gathered her wrists within one of his hands and sawed through the plastic cuffs that held her.

Kate slumped into the canvas chair and bit into an apple while she watched the small group of people move around the room, laughing and joking. The morning's training session had left her feeling overwhelmed and out of her depth.

When she'd applied for the job three months ago, it had been an act of defiance. In her mind, it was a way to move on from a messy split from a long-term relationship with a man who'd admitted to having a lengthy affair, only days after telling her he didn't share her need to start a family.

The rejection still hurt. Secretly, she hoped that by throwing herself into the deep end with such a demanding role, the pain would fade.

She took another bite of the apple and thought about the new passport safely tucked away in her bedside drawer at the hotel. The online advertisement for the role promised international travel in return for hard work and unparalleled dedication to the Business Development division of the owner's company.

She observed him now.

Ian Hart walked around the room, laughing and joking with the other new staff members who had joined him at the remote farmhouse for the survival course. An electronics engineer, he had invented a new computer circuit in his twenties which, thirty years later, was an integral part of seventy per cent of the world's surface-to-air missile systems. And he was still hungry for the remaining thirty per cent.

Using the money from the defence side of his business, he'd expanded it to encompass hospitals, universities and IT companies – the division by which Kate would now be employed.

The only concession to his notorious business drive which had been made this weekend had been for his American wife, Cynthia, to join the small group in the evenings for dinner. Kate secretly thought that as the only other female in the group, this was more for her benefit than Ian's.

Finn Scott, the man who had been interrogating her earlier, had taken up residence at the far end of the room, and despite the recent antagonism between them, Kate couldn't help watching him out of the corner of her eye as he spoke with her new employer.

She wondered what his background was – Marines? Special Forces? Federal agent? American in any case, the same as she – and a long way from home here in the wilds of the Northumbrian moors. There was *something* of the military about him, and the lower half of a tattoo poked out from the sleeve of his t-shirt, but he wore his hair longer than an army buzz cut – and no wedding ring she noted, smiling.

She broke away from her thoughts as he approached with Ian, a lazy grin on his face as he passed.

'Don't get too comfortable, princess,' he drawled. 'We'll be doing it all again within the hour.'

With that, he followed Ian out the room and closed the door behind them.

She sighed, stood, and threw the apple core into the nearest bin before joining her colleagues and tried to look enthusiastic about being held hostage by the infuriating man.

'You can't take her with you.'

'Don't be ridiculous. She's already got the job. Her visas came through last week.'

'Cancel them.'

Ian Hart threw the report he'd been reading onto the desk surface and turned to face Finn, his hands on his hips. 'Don't tell me how to run my business.'

Finn ran a hand through his hair, and began pacing across the carpet. 'She's too inexperienced. She's never even been overseas until now. She fell apart in the *training* for Christ's sake!' He turned to Steve. 'Help me out here, will you? Tell him!'

'I use your company to train my staff so they *are* ready,' said Hart. 'After that, and once we're travelling, she'll share the same security as me. She'll have an apartment in the same secure compound as the rest of my staff. Every time she leaves her apartment or the office, she'll have a driver with her.' Turning, he stepped round the desk and sat down heavily in the leather chair behind it. Leaning back, he placed his feet on the desk and watched Finn pace back and forth. 'Why are you so concerned anyway?'

Finn stopped and glared at Ian. 'Because if anything happened to her, I'd feel responsible. It's my job to make sure she's ready.'

Ian cocked an eyebrow. 'Is that so?' He stared at Finn for a second, and then smirked. 'Would you be that concerned if something happened to me?'

'Oh piss off,' said Finn wearily. He slumped into one of the armchairs which faced the desk, and ignored the other man's laughter.

'Okay, enough,' Steve Orton, Finn's boss, said. 'This isn't helping anyone. Ian, with all due respect, if Finn believes she needs more training, then you should delay her trip. She can always follow you out in a week's time.'

Hart shook his head. 'No way. She knew what she was letting herself in for when she applied for the job. She told us she was looking for a challenge.' He held up a slim file. 'Her application was impeccable – she'll be the best sales development person I'll have with me. As it is, we're scheduled to begin meetings with potential customers in London next week, and then we leave for the Continent.'

He turned his attention back to Finn. 'I know what happened to you, and why that's possibly clouding your judgement.' Ian's expression grew serious as he eased his feet off the desk and leaned forward. 'From what I've heard, it wasn't your fault.'

Finn shrugged, but remained silent.

Ian straightened up and checked his watch. 'I've got a telephone conference in five minutes. I suggest you give them another half an hour to finish their lunch, and then start the afternoon session.'

Finn growled and stood. 'I still say she won't be ready.'

Ian smiled. 'Then make sure she is.'

Halfway through the afternoon, Kate hurried over to where a tangle of gorse bushes grew to one side of the forest track and threw up the contents of her stomach. She groaned and bent down, resting her hands on her knees. The muscles in her thighs and calves burned, echoing the acid taste in her mouth.

'Here.'

She opened her eyes and an open bottle of water was thrust at her. She glared at the man holding it, then snatched the bottle from him and tipped her head back.

'Hey, steady – *steady*!' said Finn, taking the bottle from her. 'You drink like that, it's all going to come straight back up. *Slowly*, okay?'

She nodded and held out her hand. 'Give it back.'

She turned and staggered over to a grassy mound next to the track and collapsed onto it, sweat trickling down the back of her neck. She took another sip of the water, then closed her eyes and splashed the remaining liquid over her head.

Slicking the tendrils of her hair away from her face which had escaped her ponytail, she opened her eyes to find Finn watching her intently. 'Now what?'

'Don't ever waste water like that.'

'What?'

He pointed at the empty container. 'It's for drinking, not washing. You won't know when you'll get your next ration, so don't waste it. You can't afford to.'

Kate stared at him, her mouth open. A split second passed before she realised he wasn't joking. She stood slowly, and then walked towards him, waving the bottle. 'I've just finished your stupid assault course for the second time in an hour, ran two miles for the first time in five years and thrown up, and you want me to save *water*?' Her voice rose with each step.

'It's for your own good,' he said, folding his arms across his chest. 'You need to be prepared. You have to...'

'Shut *up*!'

He stepped back in surprise as the empty bottle struck him seconds after Kate yelled. He stared down at his chest then back at her, before striding across the open ground between them.

She swallowed hard, stunned by the anger that thundered across his face.

His breathing ragged, he reached out and seized her by the arm. 'You've got to start taking this seriously,' he said through gritted teeth.

She stared up at him, all too aware of the heat coming off his body and the feel of his skin wrapped around hers.

He let go, as if an electric shock had raced through him. 'I'm sorry,' he said, turning away. 'That was uncalled for.'

She watched in astonishment as he walked away a few paces, and then stood with his back to her. She took a deep breath before walking towards him.

'I'm sorry too,' she began. 'I'm not used to… to this.' She laughed, but it came out brittle, forced. 'The most exercise I get is a spin class once a fortnight – and that's only if a friend has bribed me into doing it.' She broke off as she reached him, and he turned.

'You have no idea what you're walking into,' he said.

She stood her ground and hugged her arms around her stomach. 'Tell me.'

'It's Eastern Europe. You're female,' he said, moving closer. 'To anyone that takes you, you're a commodity. Something to be bargained with. Used.'

She held her breath, transfixed as he drew nearer.

'I know you think you're a hot-shot saleswoman, but those skills aren't going to keep you safe.' His arm moved up, and his fingers wrapped around a strand of her hair which had sprung loose again from her ponytail. He twirled it in his fingers before tucking it behind her ear, and then let his hand fall. 'Get out now. Walk away.'

'I can't. I have to go,' she said. 'There's no-one else. The Business Development guy who was meant to go can't – his wife is ill.'

'You don't *have* to do anything dammit.'

'I don't expect you to understand. I – I need to do this.' Kate closed her eyes and took a calming breath to steady her voice before facing Finn again. 'I need to prove to myself once and for all that I can stand on my own two feet.' She sighed. 'There are people expecting me to fail at this, saying I haven't got the guts, and I won't let them win.'

She frowned. 'Anyway – why are you so concerned? What happened? Why are you so angry with me?'

He placed his hands on his hips, appeared to consider her question, and then shook his head slightly. 'If you don't learn anything else from this weekend, understand this,' he said. 'You travel nowhere without one of Ian's security men going with you. If you fear for your life at any time – if the pressure of working in some of the countries he takes you to gets too much, you walk away. Is that understood?'

Kate stood, dumbfounded, as Finn turned and jogged away from her towards the farmhouse, then she bent down and picked up the empty water bottle.

'Come on!' he yelled over his shoulder. 'We haven't got all day!'

She hissed through her teeth. 'Idiot.'

Kate took a sip of the wine, the rich burgundy liquid warming her throat.

After three days spent at the sparsely decorated farmhouse, the luxurious surroundings of the five-star country hotel had been a welcome surprise. After being shown to her suite and indulging in a hot shower, Kate had joined her colleagues for cocktails. Now, Hart's new business executives and their training instructors were enjoying a three-course dinner, with no expense spared.

Putting the glass down, she leaned forward on the table, caught Finn's eye and smiled. 'Let's face it, though. The chance of anything happening to us is rare, isn't it? I mean, you only have to look at the security that Ian has around him. No-one would try to kidnap someone who was that well-protected.'

Finn snorted. 'That's a typically naïve comment coming from someone who's never travelled overseas,' he said. 'And exactly what I would expect.'

He turned away as the man sitting next to him leaned over, drawing his attention away from Kate. The man murmured something in his ear and Finn laughed raucously.

Kate blushed, sure the comment had been directed at her, and played with her wine glass.

She glanced down at the dress she'd decided to wear for the final evening. Having survived the past three days, it had seemed appropriate to celebrate. She'd had misgivings the moment she'd entered the dining room and every head had turned to stare.

To her surprise, Finn had been the one to rescue her. He'd pushed past Hart, and seemed to assess every curve of her body as he'd walked towards her. Then he'd winked and kissed her cheek, before handing her a glass of wine.

Now she felt overdressed and out of place. She tucked a strand of her shoulder-length blonde hair behind her ear and sighed.

The woman next to her put a hand on Kate's arm.

'Ignore him,' she said. 'He's a Neanderthal at the best of times.' She took a sip of her wine. 'What made you apply for a job with us anyway?'

Kate shrugged and turned to Cynthia, her boss's wife. 'My ex was a bit of a control freak,' she said, fingering the stem of her wine glass. 'I guess I had enough of being bullied.'

Cynthia smiled. 'So you figured this would be a good way to prove yourself.'

'Exactly. I – I need to convince myself that I'm capable on my own.' She cleared her throat. 'Sorry – I mean, I know I can do the job. It'll be strange travelling around so much, though, and staying in different places.' She fell silent and took another sip of her wine.

The older woman smiled. 'You'll be fine – you'll be so busy you won't have time to worry about it.'

Kate laughed, some of her misgivings allayed temporarily, and put down her wine glass. 'So what will you do while Ian is travelling the world for the next twelve months?' she asked, directing the focus of the conversation onto safer ground.

Cynthia waved her hand dismissively. 'Oh, I expect I'll go back to New York eventually, oversee a couple of events at the gallery. I have to go down to London with Ian next week, so I'll pop into our gallery there to make sure everything's okay. I've got great staff running the places for me, but I like to be around for the big events just in case.'

Kate smiled politely. Ian and his wife moved in completely different social circles. She was amazed they were still together.

Cynthia appeared to pick up on her thoughts. 'Don't worry about me,' she said. 'While Ian is gallivanting around the world trying to win the next deal for whatever engineering marvel he's designed this time, I'll be making sure our houses will see at least *some* entertaining while he's away so people don't forget who we are.'

Kate heard the unmistakable tone of bitterness in the woman's voice and prudently chose not to comment further. She was saved by Ian turning to his wife and asking about her plans for the gallery while he was away, and instead tuned into the conversation to her right.

Her attention wavered as Finn's voice cut across the table. She gazed over to where he sat diagonally opposite from her. His face was animated as he described something, his hands miming in tandem with the story.

He broke off with a smile as those around him dissolved into laughter, and at that moment, he turned and caught her staring. The smile reached his eyes, the sun-kissed skin around them crinkling with humour, before he wrapped his fingers around the stem of his wine glass and silently raised a toast in her direction.

She returned the gesture and was disappointed when the executive next to Finn interrupted him and continued their conversation.

Cynthia noticed her reticence and called out to Finn. 'Mr Scott – how did the training go this weekend?'

He turned back towards them, looking at Kate as he spoke. 'As best can be hoped given the people I'm trying to teach.'

Cynthia laughed. 'You're such a miserable man, Finn. Surely you can give them something positive to work with.'

Finn shrugged. 'If they remember to keep alert and remember what we've taught them, they might do okay. If something does happen, they'll only have themselves to rely on until we find them.'

Kate put down her wine glass. 'I guess my best chance of escape will be if they move me to a different location. I can try to run away.'

Finn shook his head, and Kate noticed the sadness cross his face before he spoke. His words chilled her to the bone.

'If they move you, they're going to kill you.'

Chapter 2

Six months later

Istanbul, Turkey

Her heels echoing on the marble tiles, Kate hurried through the air-conditioned reception area. As she approached the large front doors, a security guard stepped forward, nodded, and opened one half of the oak panelling.

'The chauffeur's almost finished checking the car, Miss Foster. You might want to wait up here in the shade.'

'Thanks, Phil.'

Kate shrugged her grey linen jacket off her shoulders and tucked it in the crook of her arm while she rolled her shirt sleeves up. She sighed as her gaze travelled down to the trousers she was wearing. She'd kill for a pair of shorts right now. She stood at the threshold of the building, watching Ian's driver as he walked around the saloon car, crouching to peer underneath it, then checking the engine block and mounting. She shivered, not wishing to dwell on the possibility of a bomb being fastened to the vehicle.

The chauffeur stood and patted the bodywork, then turned and beckoned to Kate.

She slipped her sunglasses over her eyes as she left the building and hurried down granite-hewn steps. At eight o'clock, the morning sunlight already burned down from a cloudless sky, its heat bearing down on her as she left the cool confines of the organisation's temporary headquarters. She ran her hand through her hair, cursing the humidity which made it impossible to do anything stylish with it and checked her pocket for an elastic band to tie it back with.

'Morning, Miss Foster.'

'Hi, Mick. Everything okay?'

'Yeah – I checked the interior earlier. All good to go.'

'Got the air con on?'

'It's been on for the last five minutes. It'll be down to at least sub-tropical temperature in there by now.'

The driver grinned as he opened the back door of the car for her and waited until she'd settled into her seat. He slammed the door shut and then jogged round to the front of the vehicle. As he moved, Kate caught a glimpse of the revolver holstered under his suit jacket.

The car crawled away from the kerb and into the traffic, and Kate settled back into the leather seats which carried an aroma of new polish. The heavy doors muffled the cacophony of noise from the street as the car passed through the town, the market stalls and street vendors a blur of colour against the limestone walls of shops and houses that crowded the business district.

Mick caught Kate's eye in the rear-view mirror and raised an eyebrow. 'What is it this time?'

'Perfume.'

'Must be serious.'

'It had better be.'

The driver smiled, and then concentrated on manoeuvring the car through the busy traffic.

Kate checked her watch. At such short notice, she'd be lucky to make it to the boutique store from which Ian's current lover insisted he buy her gifts, before returning to the office to attend a video conference call with Hart's Research and Development department back in the States. She hadn't been made privy to the reason for the meeting, although she had gleaned enough information to realise that one of Ian's deals wasn't working out as well as he might have hoped.

She sighed, thinking back to the task in hand. His latest infatuation began three weeks ago, only days after they'd landed in the country to oversee a deal which Ian had alluded would likely double the value of the organisation overnight. Some six months and three countries later, Kate was beginning to wonder if the role was still right for her, especially when lately her boss seemed less impressed with her marketing skills and more so with her ability to choose the perfect gift for his lovers.

She wondered who the subject of his desire was this time. She and Mick had briefly discussed it, but as far as she could tell, it seemed none of the other staff knew about the affair. Ian insisted on complete confidentiality from his employees. Their contracts clearly stated the penalties for non-compliance, which ranged from being fired on the spot and even sued, depending on the severity of the breach of privacy. Together with a generous salary package, Ian knew how to keep his staff loyal.

Kate wondered privately what his wife, Cynthia, thought of his affairs, suspecting that the woman knew, but tolerated them so she could continue to live and entertain her friends in the couple's spacious household while her husband travelled the world, rather than suffer the indignity and reduced income that a divorce would entail.

Mick broke through her reverie. 'Going to take the usual short-cut here – that okay with you?'

'Sounds like a good idea. How are we doing for time?'

'You'll have fifteen minutes at the store if I'm going to get you back to the office in time for your next meeting. I'll keep the engine running.'

The chauffeur flicked the indicator and turned up a side street, the buildings on each side crowding the road and sheltering the car from the harsh sunlight. Kate peered through the window as they passed worn wooden doors set into the brickwork. Occasionally, there would be a gap between the buildings – sometimes leading through to a cul-de-sac or courtyard where laundry had been strung up between the buildings to dry. At other times, the spaces were filled with rubble where a building had been knocked down and waiting to be redeveloped. The car surged forward as Mick pressed the accelerator to the floor.

Kate turned her head to the right at the sound of a car's engine roaring towards them at speed and screamed out to Mick, but it was too late.

The other car lurched out from one of the recessed courtyards and drove straight into the side of their vehicle.

Kate heard a loud metallic crash as she was thrown sideways in her seat. The car was shunted hard with the force of the collision.

She screamed as Mick's skull smashed against the driver's window, sending blood spraying over the windscreen and upholstery. He slumped against his seatbelt. It took a split second for Kate to register that the car was out of control. Mick's foot was pressed hard against the accelerator, and the vehicle lurched along the narrow street.

She unclipped her seatbelt, scrambled between the front seats and grasped hold of the steering wheel. It felt loose under her touch, unresponsive. Her eyes opened wide. The narrow street only ran for another few hundred metres. In front of her, the narrow street ended in a T-junction, the busy main road ahead churning with traffic. Buses, trucks and cars flashed between the gaps in the buildings ahead.

Desperately, she shook the driver's shoulder. 'Mick! Wake up!'

She tore her eyes away from the blood running down his cheek and peered at the pedals. Mick's foot was jammed against the accelerator by his weight, and she couldn't reach past him to get to the brake. As her gaze tracked hurriedly through the vehicle, she realised what she'd have to do.

Swallowing hard, she wrapped both hands around the handbrake, wedged herself between the front seats, closed her eyes and pulled, bracing herself for the inevitable impact.

Kate blinked rapidly, a loud noise rousing her from unconsciousness.

She raised a hand to her head, a sticky warmth giving way to a steady trickle above her eyebrow. She looked at her fingers, at the blood, and then groaned.

She'd fallen into the recess between the front and back seats, her legs twisted awkwardly under her body. The car's engine was silent except for a ticking sound. It took Kate a few seconds to realise that the noise came from the radiator as it cooled down, its contents dripping out through the engine block. She raised her head between the seats and gasped at the devastation to the car.

The front of the vehicle had crumpled under the force of the impact – she could see now that it had careened off the narrow street, stopping abruptly when it had slammed into the far wall of a building. A laundry line had fallen onto the windshield, coloured fabrics now strewn across the glass, shading the interior of the car and obliterating her view.

She frowned. The driver's door was wedged open on its hinges, and there was no sign of Mick. Traces of blood covered the seat and windscreen.

She sensed movement behind her before the back door was wrenched open. Broken glass rained onto her shoulders. Rough hands grabbed her, pulling her upright, before they hauled her backwards.

Kate thrashed out with her hands and feet, knowing something was desperately wrong with the situation.

Voices, in the rough patois of the city, became urgent, their meaning apparent as another set of hands joined the first and wrenched her from the vehicle.

Kate cried out as her ankle caught and twisted against the door frame. Someone behind her cursed, and then leaned forward and jerked her foot until it was freed, before she was dragged from the vehicle.

She screamed as they passed the driver's door of the vehicle. Mick had been dragged from the car, his body lying prone on the surface of the road, a bullet wound to his head. Blood and splinters of bone stained the pavement. Kate realised now what the sound had been that had woken her from unconsciousness.

'Someone! Help me!' she screamed. '*Imdat! Imdat!* Help!'

A hand clamped over her mouth, and a voice hissed in her ear. She only understood the inference – to stay quiet. The surface of the man's hand scratched her skin while the scent of motor oil and salty water penetrated her senses.

She began to struggle, kicking out and wriggling in the man's arms, twisting her head to check the windows and balconies that overlooked the courtyard. There had to be someone, *anyone*, at a window, wondering what all the commotion was about.

The courtyard remained silent, save for her muffled cries, the urgent conversation between her two captors and the sound of their feet scuffing the road.

Kate's head snapped to the left at the sound of another vehicle travelling at speed. As it came closer, she bit down on her captor's hand. He cried out, loosened his grip on her, and she broke free.

Moving as fast as she could with a twisted ankle, she limped towards the entrance of the courtyard and the sound of the oncoming vehicle. She ignored the shouts of protest from behind her and concentrated on putting as much distance as possible between herself and the two men.

The approaching vehicle changed down a gear, then appeared at the courtyard entrance – a silver people carrier with tinted windows. It slid to a halt, the rear of the vehicle filling the small lane and blocking Kate's escape.

'Oh no,' she groaned, realising her mistake.

The side door began to slide open, the inside of the vehicle dark against the bright sunlight. Kate squinted, holding her hand over her eyes, then ran towards the back of the vehicle.

She began to squeeze her body through a small gap between the van and the wall of the building, using the vehicle's fender to climb up. She turned her head at the sound of a shout, and her heart fell as two men climbed out the other side of the people carrier, rounded the back of the vehicle and smiled at her. She turned and checked over her shoulder, but it was too late – the other two men had caught up with her.

Hands encircled her waist, lifting her backwards.

Kate kicked out and screamed.

One of her captors cursed as her elbow connected with his cheek. He spun her around in his arms and slapped her across the face before pushing her through the side door of the van.

Kate blinked, shocked, and then screamed as a hood was lifted in front of her face before it was shoved over her head.

This can't be happening.

She began to hyperventilate as rough hands gathered her wrists together, and she felt plastic loops push over her fingers, tightening around her skin.

She felt something soft over her mouth and nose and realised too late what was happening. She struggled one final time as the chemicals consumed her senses.

Her brain registered movement before she slipped into unconsciousness and the van accelerated away.

Chapter 3

Northumberland, UK

Finn paced around the small classroom, his voice clear, his body animated as he took the group of executives through the introductory part of the three-day survival course, explaining what the next three days would entail.

'By tomorrow, we'll be in hostage mode. You'll see on the agenda for Day Two that we've put 'leisure time'. Don't believe it. Tomorrow, stay on high alert. At any point during the course of the day, we'll be coming for you.' He paused, watched his audience react. Some appeared excited, most were worried. He smiled. 'It won't be pleasant, I know, but it's for your own good – trust me. We want you to put into practice what we're teaching you.'

He broke off as the door to the classroom opened. Steve stepped over the threshold, apologised to the executives and pushed another man into the room. 'Need you, Finn. Apologies everybody. This is Chris, and he'll be taking you through the remainder of your course.' He beckoned to Finn. 'Now.'

Finn nodded to Steve. 'Right, everyone, you heard the man. Chris has worked on numerous operations, so you're in good hands.'

He swept his notes off the table and followed Steve out the door. 'What's going on?'

'Five minutes ago we received a call from Ian Hart. One of his people has been taken.'

Finn's stomach lurched. 'Where?'

'Istanbul. There's a car leaving here in half an hour.' He checked his watch. 'That gives you fifteen minutes to pack.'

'Steve, I don't know about this.' Finn ran his hand through his hair. 'It's been a long time since I've run a rescue mission. Are you sure?'

'You can't spend the rest of your life hiding in a classroom, Finn.'

Finn exhaled. 'What about Chris? I've been out of active service for three years – he only left the army last year.'

'There's no time for this now. You're coming with me.'

Finn frowned. 'Who was taken, Steve?'

The older man checked over his shoulder before turning back to Finn. 'Kate Foster.'

Finn swallowed. 'Kate?' His mind raced. *Dammit, why hadn't she listened?*

'I'll fill you in on the rest of the details on the way to the airport, okay?'

Finn nodded, then slapped the man on the arm and jogged away from him. 'I'll be there.'

'Finn?'

He stopped and turned.

'It's not going to be like last time, okay? We'll get her.'

Finn stiffened, before forcing himself to concentrate. He nodded and ran up to his room.

His mind worked overtime as he dragged his 'ready' pack out from under the bed. He'd had a bad feeling about Kate accompanying Hart overseas, and now all his fears were realised. The diminutive

American knew how to do her job, he didn't doubt that, but she'd either chosen to ignore all the warnings she'd been given about travelling to potentially unsafe places, or Hart hadn't told her the full extent of dangers she'd face there.

Finn suspected the latter.

He packed sparsely, hoping that his time in Turkey would be short – and successful.

He swallowed. He didn't know how he'd cope if he failed.

Steve threw the last of the equipment cases into the back of the car and slammed the door shut.

As the vehicle pulled away from the house, Finn turned to him. 'Okay, what has Hart told you so far?'

'About two hours ago, the car Kate was travelling in was involved in a road accident. It sounds as if it was deliberate, rather than an opportune robbery gone wrong because the driver was dragged from the car and executed.'

'Jesus.'

Steve nodded. 'Exactly. Kate was removed from the back seat of the car. Apparently there's evidence of a struggle, so she put up a fight.'

'Local authorities?'

'Hart reported the car missing after it failed to show up at the airport to meet some guests of his. His security team found the vehicle – they have a trace on all the cars that Hart and his staff use in case they get into trouble and something like this happens.'

'What are the police doing about finding Kate?'

Steve looked down at his hands, then out the window. 'They don't know about Kate.'

'What?'

'Hart received a phone call from someone purporting to represent the kidnappers. The caller specifically stated that he mustn't report her disappearance to the police. In the circumstances, I cut him off – told him we'd be in touch, in case the kidnappers were monitoring his calls. We'll get more information when we arrive.'

Finn let his head fall back against the seat and closed his eyes for a moment. The full horror of the last mission flashed through his mind. He shook his head and opened his eyes, then turned to the man next to him. 'So how do you want to run this?'

'Let's get there first, see what the lie of the land is and go from there. We should press on Hart the importance of using the local police as soon as possible if we've got any hope of finding Kate.'

The two men fell silent as the car sped through the countryside towards the airport, each lost in his own thoughts.

Istanbul, Turkey

Finn sat next to Steve in the air-conditioned reception area of Hart Enterprises, his foot tapping the carpeted floor.

Opposite, at a glass and marble-hewn desk, the receptionist peered up from her work and frowned at the distraction.

Although the office space was temporary, rented out for the duration of Ian's stay in the country, his staff had branded it with corporate logos, glossy brochures and plush furniture, all designed to impress a potential client.

Finn winked and aimed his most disarming smile at the receptionist. His foot continued to tap on the floor.

'If you don't stop that now, I'm going to throw you through that plate-glass window,' Steve murmured.

'If Hart doesn't show his face in the next sixty seconds, I'm taking him with me,' said Finn through gritted teeth. 'What the hell is he playing at?'

At that moment, the door at the end of the corridor opened, and Ian Hart hurried towards them. 'Gentlemen, apologies – I was held up in a phone conference.'

'About Kate?' asked Finn, as both men stood.

'Um, no – I had to honour a prior engagement with a potential buyer in China.'

Finn glared at him. 'You're unbelievable.'

Steve put a hand on his arm. 'Okay, that's enough. Ian, if we could move into your office where we can talk in private?'

'Sure, sure – come this way.' Ian pushed a hand through his hair, straightened his creased jacket and led the way.

'So what's the latest?' asked Steve. 'Have you heard from Kate's captors again?'

Ian shook his head and closed the door to his office. 'No – nothing more since we last spoke. What do you plan to do?'

Finn pushed past him, dropped his bag on the floor, and made his way across to the window. He peered out, and then twitched the blinds shut.

Steve walked over to Hart's desk and turned, leaned against the polished mahogany and rested his palms on its surface.

'We'll need a room close to this one so we can set up our gear in a minute,' he said. 'We'll hook up all the incoming lines in the building through our equipment so we can monitor calls. There'll be some standard procedures we'll put in place, such as cancelling all your meetings, and I'd highly recommend that you send any non-essential staff home – I presume they all live in secured apartments?'

Hart nodded, his face pale as he realised the two men in front of him were serious. 'You want me to shut down my office?'

Finn glared at him. 'That's exactly what we're advising you do. Kate Foster is *your* responsibility. You brought her here.' He walked across the room, crouched down and pulled out an aerial photograph from his bag. 'What the hell was the driver doing turning off a main road and taking this route anyway?'

He stood and thrust the photograph at Hart, whose eyes flickered over the black circle that had been drawn around the stricken vehicle.

The man's hands shook as he held the photograph. 'Kate was, um, carrying out a task at my request.'

'What sort of task?' said Finn, ignoring the man's obvious discomfort. 'Why was she there?'

Hart dropped the photograph onto the desk and pushed it towards Steve. 'It's sensitive.'

'Try me,' said Finn. 'I'm a sensitive sort of guy.'

Hart sighed, and then gestured that the two men should sit down. He slumped into his own seat and folded his hands on the desk. 'Look, I'm not proud of it, okay? Kate was out buying a gift for my mistress.'

Finn remained silent, his green eyes flashing with anger.

'I can't go out and buy things for her myself – my other staff would get suspicious. I can't afford for those sorts of rumours to affect the business,' Hart continued, 'so Kate and the driver were entrusted with that task.' He stared at his fingernails and managed to look sheepish.

Steve broke the short shocked silence. 'How long has this affair been going on?'

'Three weeks.'

'Where did you meet her? Here?'

'Yes. She approached me at a charity fundraiser I attended when we first got here. I sent her flowers the next day,' Hart mumbled. 'It got pretty serious soon afterwards.'

'Explain.'

Hart held his hands up. 'I admit it – I've been obsessed,' he said. 'So when she started asking for presents from her favourite boutique across the city, I obliged – happily.'

Finn folded his arms over his chest. 'Sounds like she was used to get a feel for Kate's routine.'

'What makes you say that?' demanded Hart. 'What makes you think she's got anything to do with Kate's kidnapping?'

'It makes sense,' said Steve. They'd use her to dictate a routine for Kate and the driver. Every time they went to the boutique store to buy a gift, they could be monitored.'

'Did we train the driver?' asked Finn.

'No.'

'I didn't think so.'

'Why's that important?' asked Hart.

'Because we teach people to vary their route. This driver didn't, which made the car a very easy target.' Finn reached into his pocket and drew out a small notebook, then leaned across Hart's desk and plucked a pen from the collection next to the man's computer.

'What's your mistress's name?'

'Why?'

'We need to speak to her. Find out what she knows.'

'My wife can't find out about this.'

Finn raised his eyes to meet Hart's and cocked an eyebrow, waiting while he considered throttling the infuriating man.

Hart capitulated, slumping in his chair. 'Francine Dubois. She lives near Aksaray.'

'Thank you.' Finn snapped the notebook shut and threw the pen onto the desk.

Steve frowned. 'What did Kate think of that arrangement, being sent to buy gifts for your mistress? When you were in England with us, you said she was going to lead your Business Development department.'

'I don't pay her to think. I pay her to do as she's told,' snapped Hart.

'Then surely she's too busy lining up deals to be carrying out such menial tasks?'

Hart cleared his throat. 'There are some business deals which Kate isn't involved in – or aware of. It's for her own safety,' he added.

'Obviously,' said Finn, his voice laced with sarcasm. 'So why do *you* think she's been kidnapped? We've got a few scenarios to consider which we weren't made aware of until now, haven't we? Jealous husband for instance? Is this Francine married?'

'I don't think it's that, honestly,' said Hart. 'Really – it's a bit extreme, isn't it?'

'You're in Istanbul, Hart – what do you think?'

Hart squirmed in his chair and contemplated his fingernails.

'Why don't you want the police to know Kate's been taken?' asked Finn.

Hart's jaw dropped. 'Because the kidnappers told me not to contact them! Anyway, you two can find her, rescue her, or tell me how much to pay for her release. No-one needs to know, right?'

'Unbelievable.' Finn sat back in his seat and crossed his arms, shaking his head.

'Ian, you know as well as us that the only chance Kate has is for us to work closely with the local authorities. That means getting them involved right *now*,' said Steve. 'As it is, they're not going to be impressed that you've known about this for the past seven hours and haven't told them.'

'Maybe Kate wasn't in the car when it was attacked?' suggested Ian, his eyebrows raised. 'We haven't considered that.'

'Has she contacted you?' asked Finn.

Hart shook his head.

'Then I think it's highly unlikely she wasn't in the car, right?'

Hart fell silent, defeated.

'Okay,' said Steve. 'We're going to get on with setting up the communications equipment. You don't answer any phone calls until we tell you we're ready, is that understood?'

Ian nodded.

'Good. We'll check the systems here – telephones, computers, the lot. It may be that the kidnappers are monitoring your communications so we'll go through those first before attaching our own tracking devices.' Steve pulled a mobile phone out of his pocket, along with a battery charger, and slid them across the desk to Hart.

'This is a pay-as-you-go phone. You use that to contact Finn or myself. You *do not* under any circumstances use your own phones to contact us, got it?'

Ian took the phone. 'Got it.'

'Good. Finn – come with me. Let's make a start.'

The two men rose, leaving Hart at his desk, his head in his hands.

As Steve closed the door behind them, Finn turned to him. 'This stinks.'

'It does.'

'Two-pronged approach?'

'Yeah. I'll keep Hart busy to make sure he knows we're playing by the kidnappers' rules,' said Steve. 'Find out what you can about this mistress of his. I'll make a call to someone I know at Interpol here – we might need his help. Report back here in an hour.'

'Got it.'

Chapter 4

Finn checked over his shoulder, his eyes scanning the street for signs of being followed.

He registered no-one, so turned his attention to the small apartment block on the opposite side of the road. No more than four storeys high, the building was cast in shadow by the larger, more exclusive concrete towers being built on each side. The sound of jack-hammers and heavy machinery filled the air, mixed with a liberal amount of swearing from the construction workers.

He crossed the street and jogged up the short flight of stairs to the front door. To one side, a door entry system listed the tenants' names. Running his finger down the list, Finn found no-one by the name of Dubois. Francine's apartment number belonged instead to someone by the name of Altan.

Finn cursed and leaned against the thick wooden door which separated him from the apartments inside. He checked his watch, then folded his arms and settled in to wait. With any luck, a neighbour would enter or exit the building, and he'd be able to slip inside using a ruse.

His mind wandered back to the weekend of Kate's training. Halfway through the last evening at the hotel, he'd realised she'd disappeared. He'd excused himself from the conversation he'd been having with Steve and one of Ian's executives, and had gone in search of her.

Eventually, he'd found her on the terrace. She'd been lost in thought, running her necklace between her fingers while staring into the darkness.

He'd coughed to warn her of his presence, not wanting to frighten her, and she'd turned towards him.

'You haven't come to spirit me away again, have you, Mr Scott?'

He'd moved beside her, aware of the faint scent of her perfume on the breeze. 'Only if it'd stop you from going to Eastern Europe with Hart.'

She'd smiled, and he'd taken a deep breath. She'd seemed so fragile, yet strong in her conviction about her abilities.

'I'm going, Finn. We've already had this discussion.'

He'd reached out, stroked her arm, feeling goose-bumps under his touch. 'You're getting cold.'

'You're changing the subject,' she'd said.

'I'll give you my phone number,' he replied. 'From what Ian's been telling me, it's another week or so before you're due to fly. If there's anything you want to ask me – if anything isn't clear after this weekend – you call me, okay?'

She'd bitten her bottom lip. 'Can I phone you about anything else?'

He'd leaned down then, and their breathing had gradually slowed as one.

She'd gazed up at him, as if unsure. 'Finn?'

In reply, he'd bent down, cupped her face, and tilted her chin towards him.

She'd parted her lips, and he'd felt her tongue caress his, before she'd gently nibbled his bottom lip.

'Hey!'

The voice shook Finn from his reverie.

An old man stood in front of him, glaring at him. 'Yes, you! What do you want? Are you selling something?'

Finn blinked, then realised the man was holding the door open, a plastic bag of groceries in his hand.

'I, no – sorry. No, I'm not selling anything. A friend of mine told me to meet her here, but she's not answering her doorbell.'

'Heh.' The old man directed his glare towards the building works next door. 'It's impossible to talk out here. All the noise and dust. You look respectable enough. Come in.'

'Thanks.'

Finn shut the front door behind him.

'Don't you have her phone number?' said the old man, lowering his shopping to the floor.

'No. I arranged for a taxi to take her home a few weeks ago, so I have her address.' He smiled. 'I sent her flowers.'

'Ah!' exclaimed the man. 'I remember – they were beautiful! I saw the delivery man turn up with those – she must mean a lot to you. The bouquet was so big, I had to help the man through the door,' he chuckled.

'I hope she liked them,' said Finn.

'Oh. She hasn't phoned you to thank you for them?'

'No. I've been a bit of an idiot, you see,' lied Finn. 'I was hoping to come here to apologise to her.'

'I see.' The old man stroked his chin. 'Well, I'd better let you get on with it.' He bent down to pick up his groceries and turned towards the stairs.

'Can I get those for you?' said Finn, and stepped forward. 'I mean, the lift doesn't seem to be working – it's the least I could do for you after your help.'

The old man smiled. 'Why not?' He held out the bag to Finn. 'Of course, you'll be wanting me to tell you which apartment is hers on the way, won't you?'

Finn grinned. 'Actually, I know the apartment. I just wasn't sure she'd let me through the front door.'

The man laughed and began to climb the stairs. 'Come on then.'

Finn smiled and began to follow the old man.

At the first floor, he turned off the landing and held out his hand for the shopping bag.

'Next floor up,' he said, pointing. 'And good luck.'

'Thanks.'

Finn jogged up the remaining stairs and hurried along the corridor until he stood in front of apartment 4E. Catching his breath, he knocked on the door and stood with his hands at his sides, willing his heartbeat to slow.

He'd given up on anyone being home, and was about to turn away, when the door was thrust open and a woman in her sixties appeared.

She glared at him with angry brown eyes, partially hidden behind a veil of thick cigarette smoke. Her hair had been styled into a mid-length mop, dark brown shot through with grey and auburn highlights streaking the ends.

She took a long drag on the cigarette before lowering it and blowing smoke to one side.

'What do you want?'

'I'm looking for Francine.'

'Do you have her phone number?'

'No.'

'How did you know she lived here, then?'

Finn lowered his voice. 'I'm the one who sent her the flowers. I'd really like to talk to her.'

'She didn't phone you to thank you for them?' The woman's eyes narrowed. 'It would seem to me that she is not very interested in talking to *you*.' She slammed the door.

Finn held his breath. Beyond the door, he could hear the woman's voice, urgent, then falling silent.

A younger woman's voice filled the space. It began as a low murmur, before she became angry, and the older voice cut her short.

Finn reached into his pocket, removed a business card, and thought for a moment before scribbling a message on the back of it for Francine to call him urgently. He just hoped she got to the card before her mother.

He added his phone number, then crouched, and pushed the card under the door before standing and walking away.

As he left the building and returned to the car, he prayed Francine would contact them. In the meantime, he'd ask Steve to get his Interpol contacts to keep an eye on the apartment, just in case.

Chapter 5

If you can, listen before you open your eyes. What can you hear? Are you alone in the room?

The memory of Finn's voice reverberated in Kate's thoughts as she tried to calm her breathing.

She kept her eyes closed, her heartbeat thudding against her ribs. She swallowed, her throat parched. A faint metallic taste peppered her saliva, a reminder of the chemicals which had been used to knock her out.

She opened her eyes, keeping her body still while she took in her surroundings. The hood had been removed, and she was lying on a thin mattress which had been placed on the floor, a pillow under her head. Opposite, a bare stone wall faced her, its unpainted surface stained in places and wet rot visible in the corners near the ceiling. Her nose wrinkled instinctively at the smell in the room – a heady mixture of mould, aged vomit and rat droppings. She listened carefully for movement around her. When she heard nothing, she risked turning her head. Rolling onto her back, she raised her hands to rub the grit from her eyes and discovered that her wrists remained tied with plastic cuffs, her hands in front of her. She groaned, feeling the pain from her ankle creep up her leg. Carefully, she raised herself into a sitting position and surveyed her surroundings.

'Oh my god.'

Dizziness washed over her, and she fell back against the wall. She fought the urge to be sick, closed her eyes and gulped in deep breaths of the stale air. Steadying herself, she opened her eyes and blinked until she could see without blinding flashes of light streaking across her vision.

She stood, crying out in pain as her weight settled onto her foot. She bent down and lifted the hem of her trousers.

Blood seeped from a cut on her ankle, purple and yellow bruising already forming around the joint. Her shoes had been removed and her bare feet sank into the meagre bedding which covered the mattress. She wondered how long she had been unconscious.

'This can't be happening.'

Once she felt she could move without falling over, she hobbled around the perimeter of the room. She guessed it to be about four metres square. A concrete floor and stone walls keeping the interior cool. A battered ceiling fan turned lazily in the ceiling.

Without windows, the walls crowded in on her, and she fought down the panic which threatened to engulf her. The room was airless, timeless, cell-like.

She wondered if Ian had called the police. Had the car been discovered? She gulped back a sob at the thought of Mick being torn from the vehicle and murdered.

Her thoughts drifted back to the hostage training, and her heart skipped a beat. Would Ian seek help from Finn to rescue her? Would Finn be angry with her? He was the only one to have voiced concerns about her safety, and she'd ignored him.

She sniffed, blinking back tears. All she'd wanted to do was prove to her friends and family that she'd gained her confidence back after her failed marriage. The role with Hart offered an opportunity to see the world, and she'd been caught up in the romanticism of the idea of jet-setting around the globe with her boss.

Now, all the questions she should have asked at the start began to swim in her mind. How safe had she been? Had Ian willingly exposed her to danger before this trip? Was she being used in some way?

'Oh god, no,' she murmured as the walls began to encroach on her, and a rising panic enveloped her senses.

A single light bulb had been fixed into the ceiling, a metal frame surrounding it to prevent the glass being broken. In the dim light which glimmered from the low wattage bulb, she peered at her wrist, and realised that her watch had been taken from her. She had no idea if it was day or night, and began to hyperventilate.

A memory surfaced, one which she had battened down and locked away for a long time. Years. It threatened to engulf her, consume her senses.

'I can't stay here.'

She made her way back to the mattress and curled up on it, drawing her knees up to her chest.

In an instant, she was thirteen years old again. Alone. Defenceless.

'Help me!'

The walls threw her voice back to her, enveloping her in the echo. She slipped further into the repressed nightmare, the cold seeping into her bones, chilling her skin. Damp air filled her nostrils, the memory of small creatures scurrying around her feet.

She curled her toes, hugged herself tighter and concentrated on her breathing in an attempt to calm her rising heart rate, in through her nose, out through her mouth. Her fingernails dug into the palms of her hands, leaving small crescent shapes in her skin, red and angry.

A nervous hum escaped through her lips. She closed her eyes and began to sob, quietly at first, and then her cries grew louder on each breath until she was screaming. Her fingers tore at the thin blanket, twisting it in her hands.

'Somebody – please help me!' she cried.

She opened her eyes at the sound of the door to the room crashing inwards, and two men rushed in.

Kate's eyes widened at the younger of the two.

He carried a semi-automatic rifle, black and gleaming – and it was pointing straight at her. A purple bruise covered his right cheek. He began shouting at her, a mixture of the local dialect and something else, then advanced towards her and raised the butt of the rifle to strike.

'No!'

The elder of the two pushed past his accomplice, hurried across the bare floor and crouched down next to her. He placed his hand over her mouth, shaking his head.

'Missy, shhhh,' he urged, putting a finger to his lips. 'No noise!'

Kate gulped back another scream, her throat raw. She panted with the effort of keeping quiet.

The man raised an eyebrow and slowly drew his hand away, but kept his finger on his lips.

The younger man drew closer and stood over her, his body casting hers in shadow, anger creasing his brow.

The older man next to her turned to him. 'Yusuf – no. He said you mustn't touch her.' He turned back to Kate. 'You must be quiet.'

'I can't stay in this room.'

The man laughed. 'But you are our prisoner. This is where you will stay.'

'I can't stay in *here*.' She gestured to the walls. 'There's no air – no window.'

Yusuf crossed his arms and slung the gun over the crook of his arm, waving his hand at the walls. 'You are afraid of no window?'

'Yes,' she said and wiped a bead of sweat from her eyes. 'I can't stay here.' She blinked.

She picked at a fingernail, tearing it until blood trickled from the wound, and then wiped fresh tears from her eyes. 'You don't understand – I can't stay in enclosed spaces. I haven't been able to since I was a kid.'

The man sighed and turned away, beckoning the older man towards him. Kate watched as they conferred and then the older of the two turned back to her.

'If we move you to a room with a window, you must promise to be quiet.'

'I promise – please, just don't keep me in here.' She shuddered and wrapped her arms around her body.

The younger man drew closer, swung the gun off his arm and pointed it at her. 'If you are not quiet, I will bring you back here and make sure you keep quiet, you understand?'

'I understand.'

She cried out as Yusuf lurched forward and grabbed her arm before he lifted her off the floor and dragged her towards the door. From his pocket, he pulled out the hood.

'No…,' groaned Kate.

'No hood, no move,' he said, knowing what her response would be.

Kate nodded, then closed her eyes and allowed herself to be escorted from the room.

Yusuf checked over his shoulder, and then closed the door to the workshop on the lower level.

'Will she be quiet?'

'We've moved her to the front room. If she doesn't keep quiet, we'll silence her.'

'Good.' The man turned on the battered wooden stool and pushed a collection of coloured wires to one side of the workbench, before selecting one and holding it up to his face. 'I can't afford any distractions. Not now. Make sure she stays quiet.'

Yusuf squinted at the windows which covered the upper part of the walls, the afternoon sun reflecting off the dirt-strewn glass. He checked his watch, and then turned back to the electrician, noting the effort of concentration etched across the man's face. 'How long will this take Mehmet?'

'A day at best, maybe two,' came the reply. He picked up a set of pliers. 'But we need the parts from Hart. This isn't going to have the effect you want without them.'

'I'm sure with the leverage we have, we'll get the parts you need.'

The electrician lowered his voice. 'It's a hell of a risk.'

'That's the way he wants it done.'

'And if we don't get the parts?'

'We will.'

Chapter 6

Finn turned in his seat, and then rose to his feet as a familiar figure burst through the door to Ian's office.

Ian seemed surprised at the sudden arrival of his wife, but he recovered well. 'I thought you were on tomorrow's flight?'

Cynthia waved her hand. 'I told them it was a family emergency. Mind you, I had to change flights in Paris – it's been a nightmare getting here.' She shook her hair free from her scarf, fluffed it up with her fingers and hurried into her husband's arms. 'What's going on? Have they asked for a ransom?'

'Not yet.'

Cynthia sank into the other armchair. 'I knew it.' She glared at her husband. 'I told you she shouldn't be here. It's too dangerous. What if they hurt her? What if these two can't find her? It's just too...'

'I know Cyn, but it's too late for 'what if's.'

'Well what are you doing about it?'

Finn felt the woman's eyes boring into him. 'We're using the spare office next door as a command post. We've just finished fixing all of the phone lines into this office so we can monitor incoming calls.'

Ian leaned against the desk, his knuckles white as he gripped its surface. 'Finn's told the girl on reception to hold all my other calls just in case.'

'We'll tell people that Ian has been called away for a couple of days,' explained Finn. 'Hopefully they'll listen and stop phoning for him so we can keep the line free.'

'What about the police?'

'I've asked Steve to hold fire getting them involved for the moment,' Hart said, and held up his hand to ward off his wife's protests. 'Just until we know what their demands are.'

'And you're happy with that?'

Steve looked down at his hands. 'Normally I'd want them involved as soon as possible,' he said, 'but we're in an unfamiliar country and have no idea what we're dealing with. At the moment, the police are investigating Mick's death as a car-jacking gone wrong. I can make some discreet enquiries with some contacts at Interpol I have in the meantime.'

'Steve's agreed to wait 24 hours to see what demands are made,' said Ian. 'I'd prefer to deal with this ourselves if we can.'

Cynthia slapped her scarf on her thigh in frustration and stood. 'Well there's no sense in me sitting around doing nothing,' she said and turned to Finn. 'Show me where this 'command post' of yours is – I might as well help you do something until you sort yourselves out.'

Finn rose and opened the door for her.

As she passed him, she stabbed her finger at his chest. 'You'd better be right about waiting, or I swear I'll make your life hell,' she said, and strode out the room.

Finn gazed up at the ceiling and took a deep breath before he followed her.

'You already do, lady. You already do,' he murmured.

Finn showed Cynthia into the communications room.

She walked over to the window and pushed her fingers between the slats of the blinds, peering out at the pink russet hues of the late afternoon sun reflected in the windows of the buildings opposite.

Finn strode over, slapped her hand away and closed the blinds once more.

'What are you doing?' asked Cynthia.

'Making sure no-one can see into the building,' he said. 'By telling Ian not to go to the authorities, they're trying to isolate him. We don't want them finding out about us – yet.'

She watched as he wired up a set of speakers next to the blinds and then walked over to the equipment set out on one of the desks. He turned a dial, listened through a set of headphones and nodded, before placing the headphones back on the table. He caught Cynthia watching him.

'White noise. It'll help break up any sound in case anyone's waving a directional microphone at the windows.' He pulled out a chair for her and gestured for her to sit.

Instead, she inspected the wires and equipment strewn over the floor. 'What do these do?'

'We're running checks on the telephones and computers to find out if they've been compromised,' he said. 'Will you please sit down?'

She ignored him, reached into the bag slung across her shoulder, and extracted a file.

'You need to see this,' she said, handing it to him.

'What is it?'

'Just open it and see. It might help,' she shrugged. She walked past him and sat down, then watched him expectantly.

Finn sighed, leaned against the desk and opened the file.

The first pages contained a copy of Kate's extensive resume, her application for the role of Sales Manager on Hart's IT team, and the interview notes taken by the recruiter.

He thumbed through these until he found the reference checks Hart's HR team had conducted. He frowned when he turned a document over and noticed a red "security clearance" stamp at the top of the page.

'All of Ian's employees agree to rigorous pre-employment security checks,' explained Cynthia.

Finn grunted in response. His eyes flickered over the emotionally-detached text of the HR team's findings. His eyebrow shot up with surprise as he read that Kate's father was a decorated Chief Petty Officer with the US Navy, who'd been forced to take early retirement after sustaining an injury while on a training exercise. He noted that her parents now resided in Massachusetts, and that she had no other siblings.

He pushed the report aside, and then frowned at the first of a set of loose papers tucked into the back of the file.

The first was a photocopied picture of a teenage girl, the print grainy and smeared. It resembled a police mug shot except in this case, the girl's eye socket was bruised, the blue-black marking recent and ugly.

But it was the girl's eyes Finn was drawn to. The brown hue, the sadness in them, was so familiar that his heart ached.

'Kate,' he whispered.

Finn pushed the photograph to one side and found a newspaper cutting tucked into the file behind it. It was some years old, yellowed with age and originated from a small town in Ohio where a thirteen-year-old girl had been found safe after being reported missing for three days.

It appeared that a schoolyard prank had gone wrong – bullies had coerced the young girl to a disused building on the outskirts of town after school on a Friday night, and had then locked her in before running away. Each thought the other had released the girl. None of them realised their error until they'd returned to school on the Monday and all hell had broken loose.

Kate had been discovered by two policemen accompanying one of the bullies. They had found Kate collapsed from dehydration. It had taken a week in hospital to get her physically well enough to return home. The psychological effects had taken longer and had only improved once her family had moved to Massachusetts twelve months later.

Finn looked up from the file. 'How did you get hold of this?'

Cynthia shrugged. 'When I heard Kate had been taken, I got her personnel file from HR. She had to undergo a psychological assessment before doing the hostage training with you.' She pointed at the photograph. 'She told them she'd had a traumatic experience as a child so the HR team had to make sure it wouldn't affect her work.'

Finn gave a low whistle and handed the report back to Cynthia.

'Don't you want to read the rest of it?'

'No.' He turned from her and walked over to the window, staring at the wooden surface of the blinds, before closing his eyes. 'You should've told us all this before she did her training with us. I would've gone easier on her.'

He cursed.

'I wouldn't have let Ian bring her here.'

Chapter 7

Sweat prickled through her hair, making her scalp itch. Using the tail of her shirt, Kate found a corner of material which was less dirty than the rest and wiped it across her face. The last remnants of her make-up stained the material, her mascara leaving a dark streak across the white cotton.

Her throat constricted, and she fought down the urge to cry, her eyes stinging.

Outside, in the distance, a car horn blared, closely followed by another. A dog barked once, and then fell silent with a whimper, its owner's berating voice muffled. The amplified sing-song of a muezzin cut through the silence, calling a distant neighbourhood to prayer. A door slammed shut below Kate, the force of it vibrating through the floor. Voices filtered up from the street outside, then grew faint.

A bottle of water sat on the floor next to the mattress which had been moved into the room with her, and she reached down, uncapped it and took small sips. A brief smile reached her lips as she remembered Finn's face when she'd thrown the empty bottle at him six months ago. He had needed knocking down a peg or two.

He'd been infuriating the entire duration of the course, but there was something about him which had piqued her interest and wouldn't let go.

She frowned. Except that once she'd left Northumbria, he hadn't returned any of her calls. For some reason, he'd erected a barrier between them. Even when travelling, she'd caught herself wondering what could have been, had he given her a chance, a way in.

Now, his advice rang in her ears. Re-capping the bottle and setting it carefully on the floor, she noticed a bucket in the corner of the room and wrinkled her nose in disgust.

She sniffed, wiped her face again, and then pushed herself back until she was leaning against the wall.

Bare sandstone walls surrounded a concrete floor and a steel girder split the ceiling in two, plaster hanging down in places. A square window at the far end of the room had been hastily painted over, the panes of glass casting a ghostly light across the room through the white sheen which now covered them.

Her hopes had increased when she'd first been led to the room and the plastic cuffs had been cut loose. She'd rubbed her wrists, smiled at the old man, who had then grabbed her roughly by the arm and slipped a metal clasp over her left wrist, then locked it shut, smiling at her.

The metal clasp was fixed to a length of chain which in turn connected to an iron hoop set into the mortar of the wall. As soon as the door had shut, she'd tested the strength of the chain and then cursed as the links held tight. Checking the reach of the chain, she'd found that she could get as far as the bucket next to the wall opposite her mattress and to the edge of the window frame.

She made her way carefully towards the window. She could see the cloudless sky between the gaps of white paint. A crack in the glass had left a small hole, and a cool breeze wafted through the opening. The blue azure of the morning had deepened, and recalling the call to prayer, Kate realised it was now late afternoon.

Outside, a tree grew next to the building, its pungent aroma teasing her senses through the small crack in the glass, mixing with the salty air which blew through the cracks in the walls. A low structure, which appeared to be used for storage, faced the building. Several vehicles had stopped outside, reversed up to open double doors, and then had left sometime later.

The sonorous blare of a ship's horn filled the air, and Kate realised she was close to the docks. Stretching up, she peered sideways through a bigger gap in the paint until she could see the muddied water of the Bosphorus between the buildings.

She breathed in deeply, the scent of spices carrying on the air. Despite everything, she was in a better position in this room – at least there was natural light and fresh air. She shuddered at the thought of having to stay in the other room, which was little more than a prison cell. Here, she could convince herself that there was a chance she might survive her current situation.

She beat her fist on the wall in frustration and turned to face the room.

Playing with the locket around her neck, she wondered why she'd been taken. Her parents were elderly, retired, and not rich, so it had to be something to do with her work at Hart Enterprises.

She wracked her mind, trying to recall if any threats had been made since she'd first met the Harts, but could think of none.

Cynthia's time was taken up between her art galleries and socialising at parties or at home.

Ian, by comparison, was extremely measured and in control of all aspects of his life. Although he attended as many of his wife's functions as possible, it was evident that he did so to source future clients. His focus was always on business – how to grow it, how to beat his competitors, how to make more money. Outside of the business, Ian Hart was an enigma.

Kate had tried finding out more about him on the Internet when she'd found out she'd successfully passed the recruitment process and had been selected for interview. Except there was nothing. Not one scrap of information about the man's life, outside of his work or Cynthia's social circle.

She'd raised the matter at the interview, causing the human resources manager to sit open-mouthed, aghast, while Ian had laughed.

'At least I know you tried to do your homework,' he'd said. 'But you'll soon see how much I value my privacy outside of my organisation, when my wife allows it.'

And inside.

Kate couldn't help wondering if she should have asked more questions about potential threats. She knew their competition well, studied their sales and marketing tactics, always making sure Hart Enterprises stayed one step ahead. She recalled the business deals she'd helped set up for Ian. They had all been with Western government procurement departments, well within regulations, and the last one had been settled a week ago, so she couldn't imagine a disgruntled client doing this.

Unless Ian was dealing outside of the organisation.

Unless Ian had done something which had broken the law.

When they'd arrived in Istanbul three weeks ago, Hart had been more introverted than usual, and looking back, Kate realised that his usual reticence had turned into something more secretive as the days passed.

His obsession with the new woman in his life had taken over his senses, and the usual focussed man she'd first started working for had been replaced with an obsessive, secretive person who bordered on being paranoid.

And now this.

A car engine outside interrupted her thoughts. As the vehicle passed the building, she heard its radio blaring loud Turkish pop music which waned with the car's passing.

She sighed and turned back to the room, wincing as her ankle took her body weight.

Her stomach rumbled as the smell of cooking wafted through the window, and she wondered if her captors were planning to feed her.

She considered screaming again when they'd first left her, but the thought of returning to the original room, and the fact that she didn't know if anyone would hear her, gave her pause for thought.

She remembered Finn saying something about making small gains with any captors, to earn their trust, so now wasn't the time to push her luck.

For a few weeks after the survival course, she'd wondered whether there could have been something between them. The way he'd let his guard down occasionally, before putting a barrier back up between them just as quickly, had given her cause for hope.

She'd left messages with Steve, the older owner of the business, on the pretence of getting more advice from Finn for her trip. She'd hoped the ruse would work, and that he'd phone her, give her a chance.

He didn't, and instead she'd turned her attentions to preparing for her new role to take her mind off him.

She sighed and shifted her weight, leaning against the wall to ease the pain in her ankle. She strained her ears and realised that she couldn't hear any children. Wherever the building was, it was in an industrial area rather than residential, but quiet.

A ship's horn blared in the distance as it passed through the Bosphorus, and she wondered where it was going.

In the low light, the walls turned pink from the setting sun, and she could see pieces of plaster hanging from the walls in chunks, a pale blue hue reminiscent of a child's bedroom. She touched a piece nearest to her, and then jumped as it crumbled under her fingers. Her nose wrinkled at the pungent scent of mould. It was obvious this part of the building hadn't been lived in for years – not by a family, at least.

She held her breath as the sound of footsteps echoed off the walls of the concrete passageway. As they drew closer, she sat down on her mattress.

Make yourself insignificant, small, so you don't appear to be a threat to them.

She returned to her breathing exercises, keeping Finn's voice in her mind.

The footsteps stopped, and then a bolt shot back. Kate didn't hear keys, so presumed that only bolts held the door in place. She filed the information away in her head, more from a sense of keeping herself busy than any hope she had for escaping from her prison.

The door creaked open on rusted hinges, and a boy of about thirteen or fourteen shuffled into the room carrying a tray. The old man followed and mumbled instructions, pointing at Kate, then the floor.

The boy approached her warily, then crouched and set down the tray next to her. He gestured to her, then the food which had been laid out on a plate, and a fresh bottle of water which completed the meal.

She nodded. 'Thank you.'

A faint smile stole across the boy's face, before the man bent down and dragged him back towards the door, back-handing him across the face and talking loudly to him.

'Wait!'

The man pushed the boy out the door, and then turned to face her, his hand on the door frame.

Kate pointed to her ankle, which was heavily bruised and swollen. 'I need something for this. Ice. Medicine.'

The man strode across the room and bent down next to her, then reached out and grabbed hold of her leg.

She yelped, and he glared at her.

Stifling a sob, she cringed as the man turned her ankle, probing and pressing the skin. 'Not broken,' he said.

'No. Not broken,' Kate said. 'But it hurts. A lot.' She cried out as the man stood and turned away. 'It might get infected.'

His shoulders slumped, and Kate held her breath.

'I will ask. I cannot promise.'

'Thank you. Really – anything you can do...,' she broke off as the man strode from the room.

The door slammed shut, the bolt shot back into place and she raised her head.

The man had left.

She tugged the tray closer and inspected its contents. Fruit, some nuts, and rice mixed with meat, pungent with garlic and spices. Her stomach rumbled, and she realised it had been several hours since her last meal.

Chapter 8

'I really thought you and Kate would get together,' said Cynthia. 'I mean, you're both single, you have no life outside of work…'

'It's none of your business,' said Finn. He glanced over at her. 'When will you understand that? I don't want anyone in my life. I'm happy just the way it is.'

'Sure you are. How many years is it, Finn? Three since you lost her?'

Finn hit the brakes and swerved the four-by-four over to the side of the road. A truck horn blared as the traffic braked to avoid their vehicle, and then swarmed past.

He punched the steering wheel, then pulled off his sunglasses and leaned towards Cynthia. 'You never, *ever*, discuss her with me.' He glared at her, his green eyes blazing. 'You have no idea what you're talking about.'

Cynthia shrank back in her seat. 'It was three years ago, Finn,' she said quietly. 'Don't you think you *should* talk to someone about it?'

He clenched his jaw. 'No. I don't.'

He checked his blind side, slipped the vehicle into gear and steered into the traffic once more. He dropped his sunglasses back over his eyes.

'Just drop it, Cynthia. Not another word.'

'What exactly are you looking for?' Cynthia squinted in the late afternoon sunlight.

'Anything.'

Cynthia sighed and moved away from the shade cast by the four-wheel drive vehicle. 'Tell me – I'll help.'

Finn turned to her, his expression hidden behind his sunglasses. For a moment, he said nothing, and then thought better of it. The more help he had, the better chance he'd have of finding Kate.

'The local police are currently treating this as a car-jacking gone wrong. Driver shot dead. No-one else involved.'

He raised his arm and pointed to the boundary of the courtyard, now blocked off by their vehicle. 'Because they aren't treating this as a kidnapping gone *right*, they might have missed something when they were searching the area. They'd have searched for bullet casings, and witnesses to a murder, but not witnesses to a kidnapping.'

He crouched down, pushed up his sunglasses onto his head and surveyed the dirt surface of the courtyard before raising his eyes to the surrounding houses.

'People would've been too scared to talk about witnessing a murder,' he said. 'They might not be so scared to talk about a woman being taken hostage.'

He straightened and turned to Cynthia. 'Come on – let's try knocking on some doors.'

'You want *me* to speak to them?'

Finn nodded. 'Most of the men will be at work for at least,' he checked his watch, 'another hour or so. The women won't speak to a strange man who appears at their doors – but they might talk to a woman. That's why Steve suggested I brought you here with me.'

He led the way towards a set of wooden double doors to the left of the courtyard. As he pushed them open, they revealed a flight of stairs which carved through the middle section of the building.

Cynthia followed, covering her mouth and nose with her scarf, and carefully stepped over the rubbish strewn over the stairs.

'How many people live here do you think?'

'Maybe five, six families – I don't know. We'll start at the top and work our way down. Best chance we have is with the rooms facing the courtyard, but we'll ask everyone, in case they overheard something.'

By the time they reached the fourth floor, Cynthia was panting and slowly followed Finn up the last flight of stairs.

He stopped on the last step and turned to face her. 'Okay, you're going to lead this. I'll stand a little away from you so I don't intimate them. I'll be within reach if anything happens.'

'What do you mean, 'if anything happens'?'

'Nothing *will* happen – stop worrying.'

'Alright – what am I asking them?'

'Ask if they heard a woman screaming this morning. Ask if they saw the car accident. If they did, introduce me as your brother and I'll take the questions from there.'

'Okay. Let's get on with it.'

They followed a narrow passageway towards the front of the building and approached the first of two doors that faced each other. A concrete balcony between them protruded out over the courtyard.

The sound of a television show played inside the room, a child shouted and was then berated by a woman's voice.

Cynthia took a deep breath, let it out and knocked lightly on the door.

Finn stood back and leaned against the opposite wall, folded his arms across his chest and waited. He forced himself to stare out over the balcony and leave Cynthia in charge.

A few seconds passed, and then the door opened a fraction.

A woman, a little shorter than Cynthia, peered out. She appeared to be in her late twenties. She scrutinised the older woman, and then jutted her chin in her direction.

'What do you want?'

Cynthia smiled. '*Merhaba*, hello – I'm hoping you can help me.' She glanced over at Finn, then back at the woman. 'I wondered, did you hear a car accident this morning? Out there?'

The woman saw Finn, and then frowned.

'You are American. Why do you want to know?'

Cynthia's smile faltered and she lowered her voice. 'My sister was in the car,' she said. 'We think she was taken.'

The woman stared at Cynthia for what seemed an age, opened her mouth to speak, and then seemed to change her mind. 'I saw nothing.'

She began to close the door.

Cynthia put her hand out to stop her. 'Please – if you didn't see anything, did you *hear* anything? Perhaps one of your neighbours saw something?'

The woman's lip trembled, and she nodded. She checked over her shoulder towards the room, then turned to Cynthia.

'I heard screaming,' she said, then jumped back in surprise as Finn pushed himself away from the wall and joined Cynthia.

'This is my brother,' said Cynthia hurriedly. 'Please – we're both very worried about her.' Her mind raced. 'She needs medication – the people that took her might not know.'

Finn patted her gently on her back. *Well done*.

The woman sighed. 'I heard screaming, but I stayed in my room.' She gathered her shawl around her shoulders and held it tightly between her fingers. 'I was scared.'

'I understand.'

'What time was that?' asked Finn, his voice urgent.

The woman shrugged. 'About eight o'clock,' she said. 'I had just returned from taking my daughter to school.'

'What else did you hear?'

'Voices, shouting. A gun.' Her hands shook. 'That is why I did not look.'

Cynthia reached out and took the woman's shaking hand in her own. 'We understand.'

'The woman was screaming for help. I think she tried to escape – I heard shouting, then another vehicle. It sounded like it skidded before stopping. Then more screaming and shouting.' She lowered her head and carefully removed her hands from Cynthia's. 'And then the vehicles drove away very quickly.'

'Thank you,' said Finn. 'You've been a great help.'

The woman nodded and began to close the door.

Cynthia turned to Finn. 'Now what? Try the neighbour opposite?'

'That's exactly what we're going to do – keep going until…'

'Speak to Melike, downstairs.'

They both turned at the sound of the woman's voice.

'I'm sorry – what did you say?' asked Finn.

'Melike – she lives downstairs.' The woman smiled slightly. 'She is nosy. Sits in her chair all day, watching the courtyard. Speak to her.'

With that, she stepped away and closed the door, the sound of bolts being pulled across echoing in the passageway.

Finn pushed Cynthia in front of him. 'Come on.'

'What about the neighbour here?'

'We can always come back. Follow the lead first, in case we run out of time.' Finn checked his watch. 'It's going to be sundown soon – people won't open their doors to strangers around here once it gets dark.'

They hurried down the stairs and towards the apartment of the woman they'd been told about.

Finn drew Cynthia to a stop on the next landing.

'Wait. Get your breath back. Relax, or you'll scare her.'

'Okay.'

Cynthia leaned against the wall next to Finn, and patted her face with her scarf.

He turned to her. 'You did well back there.'

'Really?' she smiled. 'Thanks. Although I nearly freaked out when she started closing that door, and I knew she wasn't telling us something.'

'Me too. You ready to go again?'

'Yes.'

'Go on then – you know what to do.'

Cynthia steadied her breathing, then took two steps towards the door and knocked.

After what seemed an age, the sound of a bolt being drawn back was quickly followed by the door being opened.

A wizened face peered out, the woman's features lined and crinkled. Her brown eyes darkened with suspicion.

'Who are you?'

'A stranger in need of some help,' said Cynthia, smiling.

'Heh.' The woman glared at Finn, then back at Cynthia. 'You look too rich to need help.'

'Please, your neighbour mentioned that you might have seen my sister taken by some men this morning – after the car accident?'

'What of it?'

'I need to find her. She's very sick.'

The old woman pressed her lips together and worked her mouth.

Finn swore under his breath. He could almost see the wheels turning in the woman's mind. Easing himself away from the wall, he extracted some money from his pocket.

'How much?'

The woman's eyes sparkled. 'What is she worth to you?'

Finn sighed, folded the notes and handed them all to the woman. 'Everything,' he said.

The woman grabbed the money before he could change his mind. Then slammed the door shut and bolted it.

'*Shit.*' Finn spun on his heel and punched the wall.

'Hook, line and sinker,' murmured Cynthia.

'Shut up.'

'Maybe we knocked on the wrong door?'

'No. We had the right door. *Shit.*'

They both jumped at the sound of the door re-opening. The woman held out a piece of paper to Finn.

'Here. For you.'

Finn frowned, took the paper and turned it over. The licence plate of a vehicle was scrawled across the page in spidery, uneven handwriting.

'You,' the woman said, pointing at Finn. 'Why do you really want to find her?'

Finn looked at the piece of paper, then back at the woman.

'Because I think I love her.'

Chapter 9

Kate opened her eyes, woken from sleep by a noise outside the door.

She frowned and peered up at the window. The sky had darkened, the last of the sun's rays casting shadows across the window sill.

A faint metallic sound preceded the bolts being drawn back and the door opened, the teenaged boy balancing a tray in one hand while he carefully manoeuvred through the opening.

He pushed the door closed with his foot and approached Kate's mattress with the food.

She smiled at him. 'Hello.'

She flinched at the sight of a purplish bruise covering the boy's cheek. Moving across the room, she sat on the mattress, her hands resting on her knees as he lowered the tray, arranged bowls of food and a fresh bottle of water on the floor, and then gathered up the used plates.

'My name's Kate,' she said, pointing at her chest.

The boy glanced towards her, then away, a shy smile brushing his lips.

'Kate.' She repeated, and then pointed at him. 'What's your name?'

The boy checked over his shoulder towards the door, then back towards her.

'Halim,' he murmured.

'Hello, Halim,' Kate smiled. She pointed to the bowls of food on the floor. 'Would you like some fruit?'

The boy frowned.

Kate leaned forward, picked off a sprig of grapes and held them out to the boy. 'Here.'

He rubbed his hands on his jeans, peered over his shoulder again at the door, then nodded and took the grapes.

'*Teşekkürler.*'

'You're welcome.' Kate smiled and picked some grapes for herself, then sat against the wall.

Small steps, Kate. Nice and slow.

The sound of a door slamming shut below her room shook the walls, and Halim jumped to his feet, guilt flashing across his face. He bent down, picked up the tray and hurried from the room, his cheeks plumped out by the last grapes he'd put in his mouth.

As the bolts slipped back into place, Kate **pulled** a bowl containing a vegetable stew towards her and began forking it into her mouth, remembering Finn's advice to keep her strength up.

'No sense in escaping if you run out of steam in the first mile,' he'd said.

Finishing the food, she pushed the bowls out of the way, then stood and tested her weight on her ankle. She bent down and peeled back the hem of her trousers then wrinkled her nose at the bruising which covered her skin.

'Definitely less painful, though,' she murmured and patted the cloth back into place.

She rubbed her wrist where the metal clasp now encircled her skin.

The noise of the chain already burned into her consciousness, and she knew that if she survived the ordeal, she'd wake to that noise in her nightmares for a long time.

She gathered up the slack on the chain and began to walk around the room, letting her mind wander. During the training, Finn and his boss had told their audience to try to keep their minds active if captured and held hostage in order to prevent themselves from spiralling into depression.

She thought about her captors – so far she'd met three of them. She was sure the younger man with the gun, Yusuf, had been the one to **drag** her from the car. The bruise on his cheek **looked** like she'd managed to hit him when he'd pushed her into the people carrier. He seemed on edge, violent, and someone who she'd have to be careful around, if she was going to survive her ordeal.

Then there was the older man. She tried to guess his age and put him in his early sixties. He seemed to report to Yusuf, but still held some sort of authority in the pecking order, demonstrated by the way the younger man had sought his counsel before moving Kate to another room.

Or maybe he owned the building she was held in?

Then there was Halim. How on earth had a young teenager been caught up in this? Was he related to one of the kidnappers?

She cursed under her breath, wishing she still had her watch. Somewhere between the car and her prison, it had been lost – or taken.

Her mind snapped back to the hostage survival course. Something Finn had said about marking time. *What was it?*

She frowned, her palm against her forehead and her eyes closed while she tried to recall the classroom sessions.

Day marks.

She walked over to the window. The sill was at least a hand width above her head. Placing her palms on it, she heaved herself up and peered out through the painted glass. She brought up her free hand to scratch away a section of it, and then stopped. A freshly cleaned pane of glass would be a giveaway if any of her captors **looked** up at her room from the street below.

She traced her finger across the dust on the window sill, following the track of the sun's shadow.

Then her heart lurched. *That was it.*

Scratch a surface where the sun's rays fall, Finn had said. *Each time you're fed, make another mark. That way you'll have a rough way to tell the time of day.*

Kate smiled, surprised at how much she remembered and how much she missed Finn's voice, even if he had usually been scolding her.

She **checked** over her shoulder. With any luck, the window sill was high enough that her captors wouldn't notice the marks she planned to make. Each time Halim brought her food, she would mark the window sill along the sun's shadow, creating a crude clock.

She eased back from the window and returned to the mattress. Exercise, a way to tell the time, food and water.

Progress.

The electrician bent over the workbench and carefully soldered the wire into place.

The other men in the room watched him in silence. Most smoked cigarettes to ease their nerves, the air around them pungent and grey. A murmured comment was waved away irritably, the speaker chastised.

The electrician put the soldering iron down onto the workbench, straightened and stretched his neck and shoulder muscles. He turned to Yusuf, who was towering over him.

'That is as much as I can do,' he said.

Yusuf stepped closer, scratched his neat beard and frowned. 'Will it do anything now?'

The electrician shrugged. 'It will emit a small blast – maybe an area of a few metres, but nothing compared to the damage it would cause with the right parts.'

'We're working on that, Mehmet.'

The electrician nodded.

'And it is safe here?' the bearded man nodded towards the workbench.

'As long as no-one touches it, yes. I won't arm it until you tell me to.'

Yusuf nodded and turned to face the other men in the room. 'Alright, you heard him – stay away from the workbench – unless you want to be scraped off the walls.'

A nervous laugh permeated the room, the men's demeanour respectful as they watched the electrician tidy his tools away.

Yusuf walked across the floor of the garage towards an office which had been built into the back corner. It now served as a workspace for the small group of men, while the levels above offered basic living quarters. He pushed the office door open, and extracted a packet of cigarettes from the top pocket of his shirt. He jumped as he realised he wasn't alone.

'It goes well?'

The voice came from a man who lounged in one of the chairs, his hands moving over the electronics detritus and paperwork which lay strewn across the table.

Yusuf recovered from his shock and ignored his shaking hand as he lit his cigarette. 'It does, Mr Kaan, yes. We are ready. As soon as we have the parts from Mr Hart, we will be in a position to proceed.'

Kaan nodded. 'Good.' He stood and stretched. 'And the woman?'

'Shaken. We had to move her to the front room for now – she was making too much noise in the room we had prepared for her.'

'Is that wise?'

'I think she's claustrophobic. She understands that if she makes any noise, she'll be back where she was before. I think she will not be a problem – she seems calmer now that there is a small window.'

'Keep an eye on her, Yusuf. Don't get soft.' Kaan pointed to the bruise on the other man's cheek. 'She's already bested you once.'

Yusuf scowled. 'Have you spoken to Hart?'

Kaan smiled. 'Not yet. Let him sweat a bit. I need him to know that I'm serious about this.' A frown creased his forehead. 'He will learn very quickly that I am not the sort of person who takes kindly to people reneging on their promises.'

Yusuf remained silent and watched Kaan pace the room.

'Your men – they are reliable?'

'Yes, and keen to start.'

Kaan smiled. 'That is good to hear.' He walked to the door and held it open. 'I will make the call to

Hart. Tell your men that they will soon be martyrs for our great cause.'

Yusuf bowed his head, waited until Kaan left the warehouse through the back door, and then breathed out slowly. He closed his eyes, took a shaking drag on his cigarette, then turned and walked out to where the rest of the men were waiting expectantly.

Finn and Cynthia returned to Hart's offices in silence, each lost in thought.

Finn's mind raced. Where the hell had that admission about his feelings for Kate come from? And blurting it out to a complete stranger at that?

He rubbed his ear lobe and tried to concentrate on his driving, especially after Cynthia hissed through her teeth after one particular near miss at a busy intersection.

He drove a convoluted route back to the building which housed the offices. Once satisfied that they were not being followed, he steered the vehicle into the car park underneath.

He climbed out and waited for Cynthia to join him before locking the car and turning towards the elevators.

'Well,' said Cynthia. 'I didn't see that coming.'

Finn remained silent and touched the slip of paper in his pocket.

'Does she know?'

'I doubt it. The last time I saw her was six months ago.'

'Mmm. And that didn't exactly go well...'

'I almost called her, you know, a few months back.'

Cynthia turned to him in surprise. 'You did?'

He nodded. 'She phoned – a few weeks after the course. Left a couple of messages with Steve.'

'For you?'

'Yeah. Said she wanted some advice before leaving England.'

'You think that was true? Or was she offering you an olive branch?'

Finn stopped and allowed Cynthia into the elevator car ahead of him. He remained lost in thought as the elevator ascended.

What would he have told Kate if he'd seen her since the hostage training? Would he have warned her off, told her about his past?

Was it just the circumstances of their lives being thrown together again that made him feel this way?

'Finn?'

He blinked. Cynthia stood outside the elevator door waiting for him, a quizzical expression on her face.

'Are you okay?'

'Yes,' he said brusquely, pushing past her and striding along the corridor. 'I'm fine.'

'What have you got?' asked Steve as Finn and Cynthia walked into the command post.

Finn held up the slip of paper. 'We got lucky.' He handed over the licence plate number. 'Do you know anyone who can dig around for that on the quiet?'

'I know a guy who might be able to help.'

'Go for it.'

'I thought we weren't getting the police involved,' said Cynthia.

'We aren't,' said Finn. 'We don't know who we're dealing with yet.' He tipped his head towards Steve, who leaned against Ian's desk, mobile phone held to his ear. 'Steve has contacts in different security services – they might be able to help us. If the vehicle's been used in criminal activity before, it might be flagged in one of their systems.'

After half an hour, Steve put the phone into his back pocket. 'It's in their hands now. There's nothing more I can do,' he said.

The waiting drove Finn insane. He alternated between watching the clock on the wall and the silent phone, while he sat in a chair and tapped his foot on the carpet of Ian's office until Cynthia and Steve told him to stop, both at their wits' end with his impatience.

He wondered what he'd do when they found Kate – and what he'd do to the man who had taken her. Would she be thinking of him? Would she know he was doing all he could to find her?

They jumped as the ringing of the mobile phone interrupted their thoughts.

Steve put it to his ear and listened to what the caller had to say. He mumbled a response, then put the phone down, looked at Finn, and shook his head.

'There's no record of the vehicle being stolen or involved in any illegal activities. In fact,' he said, sighing, 'there's no trace of it all – so they're using fake licence plates.'

Finn slumped into a chair. It had been a long shot, but he'd made the mistake of pinning his hopes on the vehicle being traceable. He'd spent the last hour fantasising about what he would do to the owner when he caught up with him.

He leaned forward, closed his eyes and held his head in his hands.

Steve frowned, then walked across the room to him and crouched down. 'Is this where you tell me what's going on with you? You haven't been the same since you got back with Cynthia.'

'Not here.'

'My contact will put a quiet word around – ask some people he knows to keep an eye out for it,' said Steve. 'You never know.' He shrugged.

Finn rubbed his hands down his face and nodded. 'Thanks.'

'Now what happens?' asked Cynthia, interrupting them.

'We wait and hope the kidnappers call,' said Steve.

'What if they don't?'

The two hostage specialists looked at each other.

Finn shook his head.

Neither of them wanted to contemplate such a scenario.

Chapter 10

Finn rolled the beer bottle between his fingers, retracing an old condensation watermark on the worn surface of the bar. The beer had gone warm, forgotten after he'd taken the first gulp and had nearly retched, his nerves twisting his gut.

A ceiling fan spun above his head, the draught ruffling his hair, cooling his neck. The ex-pat bartender remained at the far end of the bar, sensing Finn's reticence and left him alone with his drink. The only other patrons in the place sat at a small table in the shadows, two old men talking in low voices and drinking coffee over an hours-old game of backgammon.

He exhaled and closed his eyes, tuning out the muffled noises in the bar. His eyelids twitched and he was instantly back in Florida, cradling her in his arms as her lifeblood drained onto the floor.

He opened his eyes and shook his head to clear the image, then rubbed his hand over his face before running his palm over the tattoo on his bicep.

He'd never meant to fall in love with Kate, but that's exactly what he'd done. The mousy girl who'd been completely out of her depth during the training, and who had so naively thrown herself into a role just to travel the world, had broken through the barriers he'd carefully built around his emotions.

The front door to the bar swung open, the warm evening air pooling into the bar for a brief moment before the familiar air-conditioned coolness returned. Footsteps approached, and then a hand clapped Finn on the shoulder.

'Thought I'd find you here.'

Finn grunted in response.

'What are you drinking?'

'I'm not.'

'You are now. If anyone was in need of a drink, it's you.' Steve signalled to the bartender. 'Couple of scotches here.' He looked at Finn, then back at the bartender. 'Better make them large ones.'

He turned back to Finn and pointed to a table in the corner. 'Get your backside over there.'

Finn slipped from the bar stool and wandered over to the table. Pulling out a chair, he slumped into it, resting the beer bottle on the table in front of him.

'I've got the phones re-routed through to my mobile,' Steve said, taking it out of his pocket and placing it on the table between them. 'That means you've got precisely fifteen minutes to sulk, grieve, do whatever it is you have to do before we go back to Hart's office.'

Finn pushed his bottle of beer aside and reached for the scotch. 'Who said I was sulking – or grieving?' he growled, taking a sip. He closed his eyes as the liquid burned down his throat. 'Jesus, you could've got the decent stuff.'

'Next time, you buy them.' Steve folded his arms, leaned on the table, and then shook his head. 'I really thought by now you'd be trying to move on.'

'Stop it.'

'It hurts me too, you know. More than you can imagine.'

Finn noticed the older man's eyes reddening and swallowed hard. 'Don't. Not now.'

'Well, when? When are you going to face up to it and get on with your life?' He leaned forward. 'It's been three bloody years, Finn.'

A cough from the table behind them silenced them. They both turned to face the old men who were watching, their backgammon game abandoned, concerned expressions on their faces. Steve raised his hand to them, smiled, then turned back to Finn and lowered his voice.

'I worry about you.'

Finn shrugged.

'I gave you this job because I thought it would help. Give you a sense of *purpose* in your life – help you heal.' He sighed. 'I'm wondering if it's done more damage than good.'

Finn looked at his hands, refusing to meet the other man's eyes. 'No, you did the right thing,' he mumbled. He cleared his throat. 'I don't think I ever thanked you properly.'

Steve snorted. 'You never thank anyone for anything, Finn, that's just your way.'

'What do you mean?'

'You're so tied up in your own life, your own misery, you don't see it affecting the people you care about until it's too late. Do you?'

Finn frowned.

'This girl – Kate,' said Steve. 'You could have been nice to her, worked with her – given her some confidence. But no, you had to belittle her, make her feel insecure, just so you didn't have to show any feelings towards her.'

A faint smile flickered across Finn's face. 'Am I that transparent?'

'Like glass.' Steve leaned forward. 'You knew you'd have to do this again someday,' he said. 'It's the worst-case scenario, but you can't spend the rest of your life hiding in the classroom. Sometimes, we're going to get asked to get people out of trouble. That's what we do.'

Finn turned the glass of scotch slowly in his hand. 'I know. I just didn't expect the first time back actually doing this was going to remind me so much of the last time.' He picked up the glass and cradled it in his fingers. 'I didn't expect to be trying to rescue another woman who disregards my advice and puts herself in danger.'

'You care about her a lot, don't you?'

Finn nodded. 'Yeah.' He snorted. 'Even if she did drive me up the wall during the training. Although now I realise it was probably all bravado, just so she could get through it.'

'Then why the hell didn't you return her phone messages?'

Finn shrugged. 'I don't know. Part of me wanted to, especially after that last night at the hotel. I really felt something there.' He took a swig of the scotch. 'But I just couldn't face the thought of losing her. What if she didn't like what I did for a living? She'd only seen the training side of things. This job, Steve, it's not easy, is it? What if something happened? What if someone had used her to get to me? Like last time?'

'Only Kate can tell you the answers to that.' Steve leaned back in his chair. 'She's braver than she thinks she is,' he said. 'Okay, she fell apart on that first day out of the classroom, but she didn't give up and go home.'

Finn stared at his hands. 'I wish she had.'

'I got the impression she's quite tough under that exterior.'

'You do?'

'Uh-huh. I think she needed to pass the course,' said Steve. 'Not just for the job, but to prove to herself that her past wasn't going to hold her back.'

'You think?'

Steve nodded. 'Yeah, I do.'

'She's something else, isn't she?'

'Yeah, she is, Finn. You only just realised?'

'We're going to lose her, Steve. It's happening again.'

The other man finished his scotch in two gulps and shook his head. 'No, we're not. You're not. We can do this.'

'I hope to hell she remembers at least some of what we taught her.'

'I'm sure she will.' Steve pointed at the tattoo poking out from the sleeve of Finn's t-shirt. 'I thought you would have done something about that.'

'What?'

'The tattoo. I mean, it's a constant reminder, isn't it?'

'That's why it's there.'

'You should get the other half done.'

Finn shook his head, threw the scotch down his throat and pushed the chair back. He pointed at the mobile phone. 'Bring that. Let's get back and see what we can find out.'

Steve stood and slapped him on the back, pocketing the phone. 'That's more like it.'

Kate leaned against the wall, her eyes closed as a breeze filtered through the high-set window and over her face.

She ran her necklace between her fingers, the pendant playing across the chain backwards and forwards, backwards and forwards. She wondered if Hart was any closer to finding her. So far, her captors had made no demands of her – no message for Ian or anyone else.

Would Ian employ Finn and Steve to rescue her? At the course, they'd given the impression they were on call if Hart required their services.

She opened her eyes. Did her parents know?

She bit her bottom lip hard, trying to stem the tears. Who would tell them? Finn? What would he say?

She slumped on the mattress, weaving the loose threads which came apart from the blanket between her fingers, then turned her head at the sound of footsteps outside the door and the bolt being released.

The older of the two men she'd seen pushed open the door, allowing the boy to enter first, a new bottle of water in his hands. He set it down next to her, avoiding her eyes, then picked up the used tray and hurried towards the other side of the room.

The man stepped across the concrete floor towards her. Kate saw that he carried some cloth and a glass jar.

He set the things down on the floor and gestured to her ankle.

She nodded, understanding, and sat so that her leg was extended.

The man took the cloth, poured some of the drinking water onto it, then added the ointment and began setting a crude poultice on her ankle, before tying off the ends.

'Thank you. Thank you,' Kate smiled.

The man smiled back, and then his hand shot forward and ripped the necklace from her throat.

Kate cried out and tried to grab it from him, but he snapped his hand back and grinned.

'You bastard!'

She didn't see the slap coming. The sound of his hand connecting with her cheek reverberated around the concrete room.

Kate held her cheek and glared at the man, tears coursing down her face as he stood and turned his back on her, swinging the necklace between his fingers. He pushed the boy out the door in front of him, the teenager's face revealing his shock at what had happened. The tray wobbled in his hands as the man followed him from the room and locked the door behind them.

Kate drew her knees up to her chin and let the tears fall, violated by the man's outburst. She'd thought he'd been looking after her when he'd tended to her ankle, but now he'd stolen the last thing which held a connection to her own world.

She cursed under her breath and wiped her eyes. Finn had told the course attendees to build a rapport with their captors, but it seemed that every time she tried to make an effort, she lost ground.

Chapter 11

Finn paced the room, his fists clenched.

He ignored Hart, who sat in front of his computer, lost in his work. The occasional *tap-tap* of his fingers on the keyboard broke Finn's reverie.

A full twenty-four hours later, there had been no word from the kidnappers. The telephones remained silent, the air in the office stuffy despite the air-conditioning, and the small group were becoming fractious.

'Have they made contact yet?' Cynthia asked as she burst into the room.

Steve shook his head. 'No.' He turned to face Finn. 'That's what's bothering me. By now, a kidnapper would be telling us his demands – so why haven't we intercepted a phone call to Hart?'

'Why? Why would they do that?' asked Cynthia.

Finn eased himself into a chair, forcing himself to keep still before he answered. 'Because they know it's having this effect on everyone. Because when they *do* contact you, you'll be ready to do anything they tell you to do if you want to see Kate again.'

Steve had disappeared at sunrise, returning with strong coffee and local pastries.

'Here,' he'd said to Finn, shoving the food towards him. 'Keep your energy levels up. We could be in for a long wait.'

Finn sipped the hot black coffee, spluttered, and then added three packets of sugar. He closed his eyes, absorbing the aroma as the caffeine hit his bloodstream, and listened to the murmur of voices in the room.

The ringing of the telephone on Ian's desk stopped everyone mid-conversation.

There was a pause, and then Steve and Finn flew into action, checking wires and recording devices within the first few seconds.

Ian's hand hovered above the receiver as he watched Finn, waiting for his signal.

Finn nodded, and then took the headphones Steve handed him and placed them over his ears.

'Ian Hart.' He was unable to keep the tremor from his voice.

'Are you alone in the room?'

'Yes.' He glanced at Steve, who gave him a thumbs-up. The communications equipment was working.

'Is this call being monitored?'

Ian closed his eyes. 'No. Do you have Kate?'

'I do. She's safe... for now.'

'What do you want?'

'You know what I want.'

'I don't know what you're talking about.'

'Honour your arrangement.'

Finn frowned, watching Hart, who had slumped into his chair, sweat beading on his forehead. His hand shook harder, and he gripped the telephone between both hands.

'I can't do that!' he hissed. 'You know that's impossible!'

'Nothing is impossible,' said the caller. 'Honour the arrangement and no harm comes to the woman.'

The caller hung up, the only sound over the microphone a faint hum of the dead line and Hart's heavy breathing.

Hands shaking, he leaned over the desk and put the receiver back onto its cradle and eyed Finn.

'Now what?'

Finn launched himself across the room at the man before Steve could stop him. Cynthia cried out as the two men tumbled to the floor, Finn's hand around Hart's throat.

'What the hell is going on?' he snarled, pinning the businessman to the floor. 'Answer me! What did you do?'

A hand grabbed his shoulder and dragged him off Hart. Steve didn't let go of him until he'd reached the other side of the room.

Finn shook him off angrily and watched as Hart climbed shakily to his feet, leaning on Cynthia, who glared over her shoulder at Finn.

'I think you owe us an explanation, Ian,' said Steve, pointing Finn to a chair away from the desk. 'Now.'

Hart coughed, waved his wife away and stepped round his desk, sinking into the leather seat which creaked under his weight.

'It's nothing, really.'

'I doubt that,' said Steve. 'Not from the conversation I heard. Enough bullshit, Hart. Talk to us.'

'What's really going on here?' asked Finn. 'What's the real reason you don't want the police involved? What have you done?'

Hart rubbed his hand over his eyes before looking across at the two men and tried to avoid his wife's angry glare.

'I backed out of a business deal last week, after I found out the other party weren't legitimate buyers.'

'You need to tell the authorities,' said Steve. 'This is crazy – you're way out of your depth and we could really use their help.'

Hart shook his head. 'No – we can't. He said he'd kill Kate if I went to the police.'

'How were you approached by him in the first place?' asked Finn, turning to Hart. 'Did you initiate the contact, or did he?'

'He did. I'd secured a deal with the Turkish authorities a few months ago – they'd agreed to pay for the research and development to complete the equipment I'd been designing.' He shrugged. 'Normally the British or Americans would be the first to get involved, but there's been so much scrutiny within both governments over defence spending that they weren't interested this time.'

'What are you developing for the Turkish authorities?'

'We've designed and built parts for a new rocket-propelled grenade launcher for the Turkish army. It's not very different from the ones they already use – we're just helping them bring their hardware into the twenty-first century at an affordable cost.'

'Enough of the sales bullshit,' said Steve. 'What's the difference between the old equipment and what you've built?'

The businessman sighed. 'The parts enable the grenades to be converted into a standalone bomb. No launcher required. They also create a better spread of destruction – broader reach.'

Steve shook his head. 'Like we need better ways to kill each other.'

Hart became defensive. 'It's at the cutting edge of military technology!'

Finn waved his hand impatiently. 'What happened?'

'About six months before we were due to come out here to finalise the deal, a man called Claude van Zant contacted me.'

'How?' Finn crossed his arms and leaned against the wall.

'By telephone initially. He said he was in London for a meeting, so I met him for lunch. He sounded legitimate, but when I got back to the office, I tried to look him up on the internet.'

'What did you find?'

'Absolutely nothing.'

'When did things start to go wrong?' asked Steve.

'He phoned the week before we arrived. I questioned why I couldn't find anything about him, and he started going on about how his organisation was dependent on my help for their cause.' Ian shrugged. 'I put two and two together, and told him I wouldn't be proceeding with the deal.'

'How did he take it – before Kate was taken I mean?'

'Angry. Unreasonable. He told me I'd regret my decision and that he could make me a very rich man.' Hart loosened his tie and slumped into his chair. 'I backed down a bit, told him I'd see what I could do – I thought I'd play along, give him the impression I might be swayed, see if I could find out more about him, or what he was planning.'

'That was the point at which you should have approached the police in the UK,' said Finn. 'If you were afraid of the repercussions to your business, you could've reported it anonymously, you do realise that?'

'I do now,' Hart said, running his hand through his hair. 'I wish I had.'

'When did you find out about the weapon he was planning to put the new parts in?'

'Last week, he phoned me at the office to ask if I'd reconsider. I asked him outright what use the parts would be to him, when they'd been specifically designed for a grenade launcher. He said that he was building something which would define a new age in the politics of eastern Europe.' Hart stopped and reached across his desk for a glass of water. He drank deeply before setting the glass back down. 'He must have a source in the military too, because only two people within the Turkish army's procurement team know about these parts.'

'What did you say to him?'

Hart shook his head. 'I didn't – I hung up. I was scared about who might be listening.'

Steve had been pacing the room while Ian spoke. 'What are your thoughts, Hart? What's he planning to use the parts for?'

Hart shrugged. 'There's only one possibility,' he said. 'He's building a bomb.'

Kaan ran his hand along the workbench, his fingers leaving a path between the cast-off ends of wire, screws and hand tools.

As he drew closer to the electrician's handiwork, he turned his head slightly.

'You are sure this will work, Mehmet?'

'Yes, yes I am,' said the electrician. 'All we need are the special parts from Mr Hart, and you will have your weapon.' He fell silent, wringing an oily cloth between his hands, and bowed his head.

'Yusuf – you are happy with this man's work?'

'I am,' said Yusuf. 'He has worked diligently and without complaint. He is an asset to our cause.'

Kaan nodded, and then turned to face the room. He rubbed a hand over his chin before raising his gaze to the men staring at him.

'In less than a week, we will show our Turkish masters what we think of their efforts to join us to Europe,' he said. 'For too long, we have allowed our government to dictate what they believe is right for us.' He laughed. 'By aligning our beautiful country to a bankrupt continent, we are *enslaved.*'

A low murmur of assent filled the space, the men nodding, urging Kaan to continue.

'You are the trusted few who can change this,' continued Kaan, building the fervour which permeated the group. He held his breath, waiting until he had their full attention.

'Tell us, Kaan,' urged one of the younger men, his eyes wide with anticipation.

'Yes, tell us! Tell us!'

Kaan held up his hand until the men had settled once more, their voices reduced to a low murmur.

He stepped towards a wooden crate, slipped the lid off, and reached inside.

'Istanbul is enjoying a new age of construction and renovation,' he said. He turned, lifting a high visibility shirt and a hard hat into the air. 'What better disguise than to blend in with the workers which fill our city?'

'In less than a week, we will attack the Marmaray rail tunnel which runs under the mighty Bosphorus,' he continued. 'We shall tear apart Asia and Europe once more. We will send a clear message to our masters that we will *not* stand by and watch as they try to erase our Persian heritage!'

Kaan smiled, sweat beating on his forehead, as his men erupted as one, shouting and calling his name.

'This will be our day!' he called out. 'We will remember this day and tell our grandchildren for years to come!'

Chapter 12

Finn sat on the floor of the room he and Steve had commandeered for their use, a swathe of paperwork strewn around him.

Knowing that van Zant had approached Hart directly led Finn to believe that the bomb was being made somewhere in the city. If what Hart had said was true, van Zant was intent on using it to create an impact.

While Steve coached Hart through what he needed to say when van Zant phoned back, Finn began to try and locate the bomb.

Hart had instructed his security detail to help in whatever way they needed. Steve had reviewed the map of the city, using his contact at Interpol to identify all the low-key electronic appliance stores

Hart felt van Zant would need. Then he had mobilised the security team.

The trick was to remain low key, which was why Steve's contacts only provided information, not feet on the ground to help with the search. Hart's security team, dressed in casual clothing, were less likely to raise suspicion.

'Gently does it,' Steve had said to Finn. 'We need answers, but we can't afford to push too hard for them and alert van Zant.'

Each man had been assigned electrical stores within a specified radius within the city – small, out of the way stores off the main streets.

Now, a few hours later, Finn put down the notes and turned to the report which Steve had collated while the private security contractors were scouring the city. Steve had analysed the trace elements recorded for each bomb attributed to terrorism groups in the country. If he was right, van Zant's bomb-maker would go shopping for the same parts. Not from one electronics store, but from several in order to disguise what he was doing.

Finn worked on the hunch that the electrician would source his goods from different stores, but ones within a radius of wherever the weapon was being built. If he was right, then the purchases would lead like a trail of breadcrumbs to the bomb-maker's location.

And if he was lucky, to Kate.

Finn closed his eyes, pinched the bridge of his nose, and forced himself to focus. He cursed. He'd lost concentration, skimming through the last of the notes.

He cricked his neck and started again. Hart had told them what to look for – specific wiring, transistors, timing mechanisms. Simple things which could be purchased in any home electrical store but which, if assembled correctly, with the right mix of chemicals added, could have the potential for a lethal bomb.

And then the kidnappers were planning to enhance that with the parts they were trying to get from Hart.

From the adjoining room, he heard Steve's mobile phone ring, then a murmured conversation. He frowned and checked over his shoulder towards the door at the sound of the man's voice growing louder with excitement, until he could bear it no more.

Standing, he walked through to the other room where Steve was pacing. He turned when Finn entered the room and grinned, putting his thumb up in the air.

Finn waited until the call was ended.

'What was that all about?' he asked.

Steve exhaled, and tried to calm himself before speaking. 'That was my contact,' he said. 'Our missing vehicle turned up this morning.'

'What, abandoned?'

Steve smiled. 'No – it's in perfectly good condition. It's been moved since, so they're going to check traffic cameras to see if they can spot where it went.'

'What area is it in?'

'Haydarpaşa. Near the old port terminal.'

'It's mainly industrial around there – warehousing and factories.' Finn frowned. 'It rings a bell. Hold on.'

He dashed through to the other room and began pawing through the notes he'd already checked, his heart racing as he pushed his hands through them, his eyes scanning the addresses at the top of the documents.

A blue slip of paper reached the surface, and he grabbed it, looked at the address along the top, and then the list of parts that Hart had given to him as a guideline.

His heart thudding in his chest, Finn hurried through to where Steve was waiting. 'Might have something,' he said.

Finn parked the car a few hundred metres down the road from the shop, climbed out and leaned against the vehicle to get his bearings.

The electrical store was on a busy road, one side of which housed a string of food outlets, cafes, a tobacconist, and a small convenience store. Everything a worker might need before heading to one of the factories or warehouses that surrounded the sprawling industrial estate.

The store was squashed in between a coin laundry and a small pharmacy. Finn began walking towards it, forcing himself not to rush straight in, but to walk past it before doubling back, to make sure he hadn't been followed from Hart's office.

Satisfied, he approached the electrical store and pushed the door open. A blast of cold air brushed against his face as he crossed the threshold, an old air-conditioning unit rattling above his head as he passed under it.

He closed the door, tucked his sunglasses into the neck of his shirt, and peered into the gloom of the shop.

A counter ran the length of the store. Behind it, a variety of boxes filled with different electrical gadgets lined a shelf. More shelves ran in rows towards the back of the store. In front of the counter, refrigerators, dish-washers and ovens had been arranged in aisles, stretching across the width of the shop.

Finn wandered amongst the aisles and shelves, picking up boxes of parts and briefly reading the packets before returning them to their place. All the time, his eyes roamed the store, making sure he was the only customer.

He'd timed it well. It was early afternoon, and most workers had finished their lunch and anyone who would have called into the store during their break were now gone.

An electronic bell had sounded as he'd opened the door and now a man hurried down the length of the counter from the rear of the shop, wiping his hands on a towel.

'Can I help you?'

Finn smiled, walked towards the counter and pulled out the notes from his shirt pocket. 'I hope so, yeah.' He checked over his shoulder to make sure the door was closed. 'I'm hoping you might be able to tell me what these parts might be used for.'

The store owner slipped reading glasses off his forehead and perched them on the top of his nose. Finn noticed how the man's arm moved the page as his eyes tried to focus, and wondered if he was due for a new prescription.

'Ah. Yes.' The man slipped the glasses off his face and tapped them on the papers. 'These are quite hard to get hold of.' He visibly preened. 'I do believe we're the only store on this side of the city that stocks them.'

'What would someone do with those parts – what would they use them for?'

'Off the top of my head, if I bought these, I'd be making some sort of timing mechanism.' He frowned, and tapped his glasses on his cheek. 'Maybe, with the businesses around here, he wanted the parts for unlocking a door at a particular time – maybe to keep staff out when he wasn't around, you see?'

Finn nodded. 'Got it.'

He spun round at the sound of the door opening and was surprised to see a boy of about thirteen or fourteen in school uniform rush through, slam the door behind him and run to the back of the shop. Minutes later, he appeared behind the counter, a grin on his face and a cold can of drink in his hand.

'This is my son, Osman,' said the store owner, and Finn noticed the note of pride in the man's voice.

'Sorry, I'm being rude,' he said. 'My name's Finn.'

The man shook his hand. 'Mazhar Kadír.'

Finn leaned over the counter and solemnly shook hands with Osman before turning back to Kadír.

'So you're saying these parts aren't normally in high demand.'

'That's right. We don't often sell them. Your friend was in here earlier? The one that gave you this?' The store owner held up the notes.

'That's right. We're trying to find the man who bought them.'

The store owner nodded. 'I remember this man.'

Finn's eyebrows shot up. 'You do?'

'The man who bought the parts was very rude to my son.' A smile appeared. 'You could say he left a lasting impression.'

Finn smiled politely. 'It takes all sorts.'

'I know who he is.'

Finn nearly gave himself a whiplash at Osman's voice. He managed to keep calm, not wanting to scare the kid.

'You do?' Finn turned to Kadír, who shrugged, and indicated to Finn he should continue. 'How?'

'His son goes to the same school as me. Sometimes.' The boy fell quiet for a few seconds, and then seemed to change his mind. 'I haven't seen him for a few days.'

'Do you think he's on holiday?'

The boy took a sip from his can of drink.

Finn felt like an age passed while he watched Osman swing his legs back and forth as he sat on the stool. It took all his resolve not to leap over the counter and shake the information out of the kid.

'Maybe,' he said eventually, leaning forward and putting the empty can on the counter. 'Or he's sick.'

'Why would you say that?' asked Kadír. 'Is there something going round the school?'

'No. But sometimes he comes to school with bruises on his face.'

Finn and the store owner exchanged a glance.

'Has he lived here long?'

'I've seen him around before, but he only started in my class this term.'

'That was six weeks ago,' added Kadír.

The boy slipped from the stool and wandered back into the depths of the store. Finn heard a door slam shut and an extractor fan began to whir. He turned back to the store owner.

'Do you think he knows where the man and his son live?'

'Maybe.' The store owner shrugged.

Here we go again, thought Finn. He reached into his pocket, his fingers touching the money folded there. He carefully flicked through the notes until there was a quarter of the total between his fingers this time and extracted his hand.

'I could pay you for his time to show me,' suggested Finn. 'To make up for him not being here to help you for the next hour.'

The man's eyes narrowed. 'Why do you want to find this man so badly?'

Finn thought for a moment. He didn't really want to advertise why he was here, but given the store owner seemed friendly enough, and had obviously taken a dislike to the man he sought, he figured it was worth the risk.

'My friend was taken yesterday. Kidnapped after a car hijacking went wrong.' He pointed to the notes. 'I think that man knows where she is.'

The store owner nodded and took the money. 'That seems to be very reasonable.' He flicked through the currency before tucking them into his shirt pocket. He handed back the notes to Finn, but didn't release them immediately. 'There is no danger in this for my son?'

Finn pulled the papers out from the man's fingers. 'You have my word he'll come to no harm,' he assured the man.

Kadír nodded and they both turned at the sound of a toilet flushing. The boy reappeared and jumped at a shout from his father.

'Osman – please go with this man and show him where your school friend lives. Can you do that?'

The boy nodded. 'Sure. No worries.'

Kadír waved him away and turned to Finn. 'At least if he's with you, he's not watching the television in the office and quoting Australian soap operas,' he muttered.

Finn laughed. 'I'll bring him back within the hour,' he said and held out his hand. 'Thank you for your help.'

They'd only been driving for five minutes and already Finn wished the kid would shut up. An incessant stream of conversation left the boy's lips – television, computer games, music.

He began to tune out the words, listening only for directions as the boy called them out.

Osman cried out suddenly.

'Here! Turn here,' he said, pointing.

Finn hit the brakes and swerved into a street on his left-hand side. 'How far up the street is the house?'

The boy shook his head. 'It's not a house.'

'What?' Finn ignored the smug expression on the boy's face and counted to ten. 'What do you mean it's not a house?'

'It's a garage. Motor vehicles.' The boy jutted his chin to the right, having the sense not to point. 'There.'

Finn took his foot off the accelerator and looked to where Osman indicated.

The garage was decades old, the signage in need of a coat of paint. Two car wrecks were parked on the forecourt, while three rusted sedans were parked to the left of the closed double garage doors, the windows displaying sale prices.

Finn had time to take in the rusted window frames, the glass covered with white paint. Two levels of living accommodation or offices appeared to be above the main workshop. He lifted his gaze and noted the television aerial and satellite dish.

Business might not be doing well, but there was nothing wrong with the communications to the outside world.

Finn brought his attention back to the road and gently pressed the accelerator.

He wondered which room Kate might be in, and shook his head to clear the thought. He had to concentrate. He only had one chance at this.

Osman's voice broke his thoughts.

'Turn around here. It's a dead end if we go any further.'

Finn braked, reversed into a deserted warehousing complex and turned the vehicle around.

'Talk to me as we drive past again,' said Finn. 'Don't look at the garage.'

'Okay.'

The garage drew nearer. Finn chewed the inside of lip and kept his head facing forward, while his gaze wandered over the building.

An alleyway led down one side, and he noticed an industrial-sized waste bin overflowing onto the floor. On the other, a pathway led to what appeared to be an entrance to an office, before reaching a dead end.

'I don't think it's very busy,' said Osman as they drove past. 'There aren't many cars there. My father's business is very successful,' he added. 'Always people in the shop.'

Finn smiled at the boy. 'Your father is a nice man,' he said. 'If the man that owns that garage is as rude as your father says he is, that's probably why his business is struggling.'

He glanced in the rear view mirror, checked he wasn't being followed, and then increased his speed.

'Alright, Osman, let's get you back home. You've been really helpful, thank you.'

'What are you going to do?'

Finn shook his head. 'I don't know. But you need to stay away from here now, okay?'

The boy nodded his head. 'Okay.'

'What's your friend's name?'

'Halim,' said the boy. 'Halim Rizman.'

Chapter 13

Kate raised her head as the door to her prison opened.

'Get up.'

The younger of the kidnappers, his gun slung over his shoulder, advanced towards her. He reached down and hauled her off the mattress.

Kate instinctively tried to jerk away from him. 'Where are you taking me?'

Yusuf ignored her, grabbed her arm and extracted the hood from the back pocket of his jeans.

Kate began to struggle, digging her heels into the concrete floor, and made her bodyweight as heavy as possible.

Yusuf leaned down and grabbed her hair, pulling it hard. 'Stay still,' he said, shaking her. 'You have a meeting to go to.'

Kate's hands flew to her scalp as she tried to stop the man tearing her hair out by the roots. 'Where? Who?'

'Come with me.'

His grip on her hair weakened, and she sighed with relief, and then gasped as he slipped the hood over her head. Immediately, she began to hyperventilate.

She felt Yusuf's face move closer to hers and forced herself not to move.

'No screaming,' he said. 'You know what will happen if you scream?'

She nodded her head. No way was she going back into the windowless room.

He took hold of her arm, unfastened the metal clasp and wound a rope around her wrists before leading her out of her room. Kate tried not to panic, concentrating instead on breathing through her mouth to avoid the musty smell of the hood.

Even if you can't see, Finn had said, *you can still* hear *what's going on around you.*

Yusuf pushed her to the left as they exited the room. Kate stumbled with the sudden change in direction, and the man muttered as he dragged her up so she didn't trip and fall. She slowed down, forcing him to take his time. The last thing she wanted was to get hurt trying to keep up with him when she couldn't see where she was going.

He stopped suddenly and could tell by the shift of his hand on her arm that he'd turned towards her.

'We are going down some stairs,' he said. 'Put out your right hand. Hold onto the rail.'

She fumbled around with her hand until she found the metal surface of the rail and wrapped her fingers around it.

'Go.' He led her down the stairs without another word, moving slowly so that Kate could find her bearings with her feet each time.

Even though she only counted two flights of fourteen steps with a small landing between them, the descent seemed to take forever.

At the landing, she stopped, giving the impression she needed a rest. In reality, she wanted a few precious seconds to get her bearings, but she heard no voices on this level, no movement.

The man pulled her onwards, down the second flight of stairs. At the bottom, he picked up the pace again, turned right and steered her through another door.

She sensed movement in the room, the distinctive *chink* of glass. The scent of cigarettes wafted through the material of the hood, and she coughed.

She felt a hard surface next to her right thigh, then her body was turned and the man put his hand on her shoulder.

'Sit.'

Kate stumbled. With the rope around her wrists, she had no way of reaching behind to check where the seat was. Her heart pounded as the man pushed her down, until her bottom found the chair which had been placed there for her.

She lowered her head and waited, her bound hands in her lap.

The hood was whipped off her head, and she blinked in the sunlight which bathed the room.

The chair had been placed in front of a table. She raised her head and stared at the man sitting opposite her.

He was dressed in a suit, the sleeves slightly creased, and an open-necked shirt. A tie lay folded on the table next to him. A day's worth of stubble covered his jawline and dark eyes studied her from under hooded lids. A cigarette stub burned between his fingers, yellow nicotine stains on his nails.

A decorative teapot and two glasses, together with an ashtray, a newspaper and a mobile phone, were set out on the table in front of him.

He remained silent as he watched her, his gaze running up and down her body until she turned away, embarrassed.

You're just a commodity, Finn had said. *Something to be bargained with.*

She closed her eyes. She'd never felt so naked under someone's gaze.

'Look at me.'

She breathed out and raised her head to meet his stare.

'You,' he said, pointing his finger at her, 'are going to help me secure a business transaction.' He smiled. 'You are good at *business*, yes?'

Kate's mind raced. Who was this man? Why was he holding her hostage?

'Answer me!' His fist slammed down onto the table, making the tea glasses shake and clink together.

Kate's heart lurched at the sudden outburst. 'Y-yes. I think so,' she stammered.

He leaned back in his chair and appeared to relax a little.

Kate tried to steady her breathing, but she was terrified. The man was obviously the one in charge of whatever group her kidnappers belonged to.

The younger man who had brought her into the room was standing by the door, his rifle slung across his arms. His whole body stood rigid, poised, and he seemed in awe of the man who sat opposite her.

'You, Miss Foster, are very valuable to me at the moment,' the man in charge said.

His voice was educated, with very little trace of the local accent. He sounded as if he'd spent time in England.

She frowned as she tried to guess his age. Realising she shouldn't antagonise the man and make her situation worse, she forced a smile.

'It seems a bit unfair that you know my name, and I don't know yours,' she said, her voice shaking.

He shrugged. 'My name is Kaan,' he said. 'But you are from America, yes?'

She nodded.

'Then you will not have heard my name – yet.' He drew on the cigarette, and then blew the smoke towards the ceiling before appraising her once more. 'But your people will. In time.'

Kaan smiled, and Kate shivered. His coal black eyes taunted her, and she saw no mercy in his gaze.

'Why am I here? Why am I being held prisoner?'

'Your boss reneged on an agreement with me,' he said. 'I have no argument with you.' He leaned forward and stubbed out his cigarette in the decorative ashtray on the table. 'However, your life depends on the successful outcome of my business deal with Mr Hart.' He sighed and lifted his hands, palms up. 'Unfortunately, Mr Hart is being very difficult to deal with at this time.'

Her life? Kate's stomach clenched and bile rose in her throat.

'I have no idea what you're talking about,' she said. 'But if it's got nothing to do with me, then let me go.'

Kaan laughed, the sound echoing off the walls before his face grew serious. 'I am afraid I cannot do that.'

She bit her bottom lip, forcing herself not to beg. 'What do you want from me?'

He smiled. 'That's more like it.' He stood, then peeled the suit jacket from his shoulders and hung it over the back of his chair.

He moved around the table, rolling up his shirt sleeves as he walked, until he was standing next to her.

Kate swallowed and kept her eyes facing forward.

He pushed the newspaper towards her. 'Pick this up.'

She lifted her bound hands until her fingertips could twitch the newspaper closer, and then did as she had been told.

'Hold it so the date is facing out.'

Kate complied, feeling sick to her stomach.

Proof of life, Finn had told her. *At some point, they're going to have to tell the outside world that they have you and that you're still alive.*

Kaan walked back round the desk, picked up the mobile phone and pointed it at her.

She blinked and moved her head as the flash blinded her. When she opened her eyes, she saw Kaan checking the photograph.

'Perfect,' he murmured, before turning his attention towards the man standing at the door.

'Take her back.'

Kate gritted her teeth as the hood was pulled roughly over her head, and she was hauled from her sitting position.

'Quiet.'

Yusuf led her back through the door and along the passageway towards the stairs.

Kate strained her ears as she shuffled along.

She heard the man who called himself Kaan walk behind her. As the man with the rifle dragged her to the left and began leading her up the stairs, she heard Kaan continue walking straight on.

Kate heard a door open and stopped on the stairs, pretending to lose hold of the stair rail, while she listened.

Beyond the door which Kaan had walked through, she heard voices, the sound of a hammer knocking against something metallic. A waft of aromas assaulted her senses but one stood out from the rest.

Motor oil.

The same smell as the man's hands which had pulled her from the car.

The door behind her slammed shut, and she grabbed hold of the stair rail.

'Move,' said Yusuf.

Once back in her room, the hood removed and alone again, Kate mulled over what she'd heard and smelled, while she toyed with the metal clasp around her wrist.

A hammer on metal, the motor oil...

Was she being held above a garage workshop?

She shook her head, angry with herself. 'Can't be,' she murmured. 'There would be more cars around. There aren't any customers.'

She paced the room while her mind worked. Maybe it *was* a workshop, but they were making something else.

What?

She sighed, made her way over to the mattress and sank onto it. She reached over, uncapped the bottle of water and drank four large gulps, then curled up on the mattress and lay on her back, staring at the ceiling.

She wondered what Ian would do when he received the photograph Kaan had taken, and then her stomach churned.

Would Kaan send it to her parents? He couldn't be that cruel, surely.

She shook her head and tried to clear the thought. Somehow, she believed Kaan wouldn't send the photograph to her parents. For some reason, he didn't want the outside world to know about her disappearance, just Ian.

What on earth was he up to?

Chapter 14

Ian Hart rubbed his eyes and leaned closer to the computer screen.

Cynthia had insisted they return to the apartment so they could freshen up. While she was showering, Ian remained in his office, trying to distract himself with spread sheets and design calculations. He glanced down at his crumpled suit and realised it was nearly two days old.

Finn had handed him a mobile phone that had been connected to the office phone lines in case the kidnappers tried to contact him. He eyed it warily, afraid of what would happen if it did ring. His mind worked in circles.

If only.

If only he could wind the clock back, turn down van Zant's offer right at the start of all this. If only he'd gone to the police as soon as the threats had started. They'd have taken it seriously, especially with his line of work and the heightened security levels permanently in place across America and Western Europe.

If only he'd listened to Finn Scott six months ago, when the hostage trainer had cautioned against taking Kate with him.

If only he'd resisted Francine's attention.

He raised his head from the paperwork at a knock on the door, frowning at the interruption.

'Come in,' he said, pushing the documentation and Finn's mobile phone into a desk drawer. He failed to contain the fear which twisted his gut when the door opened and his housekeeper showed a man wearing a pale grey suit into the room.

'I'm sorry, Mr Hart,' she said. 'I know you said there were to be no visitors, but Mr van Zant was very insistent that he see you without an appointment.'

The visitor smiled. 'I hope you don't mind, Ian.'

Hart rose, his mind swirling. 'No, not at all.' He walked over to the man, and they shook hands.

As his visitor loosened his grip, Hart swallowed and wiped his damp palm across the crease of his linen trousers.

'Would you like me to make some tea, Mr Hart?'

'No thank you, Chrissie – that'll be all.'

The housekeeper nodded and left the room, closing the door behind her.

'What the *hell* are you doing?' Hart glared at the visitor. 'I told you never to come here.'

The man smiled benevolently. 'Ah, but there is so much to talk about, isn't there? Better to meet face-to-face than a phone call at the moment, don't you think?'

Hart gritted his teeth. 'You bastard.'

'Sit down. We have some things to discuss.'

Hart sank into his chair, a look of defeat in his eyes.

Van Zant smiled and reached into his jacket pocket. 'I'm going to give this to you. A reminder of what's at stake here. Maybe that will help you focus.'

A moan escaped Hart's lips when he saw the photograph.

Kate's face bore a red welt where she'd evidently been struck. Her blouse was torn, her hair matted, and there was a nasty cut above her left eyebrow, but it was the expression in her eyes...

Terrified. Fearful. *Desperate*.

He pulled a handkerchief from his pocket and dabbed his forehead as he fought down the wave of sickness which engulfed him.

'Who are the two men working for you?'

'Two men?'

'Please, Mr Hart, don't play games with me. You are not a stupid man, I know this. Who are they?'

Ian crossed his hands on the desk, realised the trembling in his fingers would only please the man in front of him, and let his hands fall into his lap. 'They are employed by the business at the request of my insurers,' he said. 'They train my staff in security techniques so that they can deal with kidnapping situations.'

'Ah. I see.' Van Zant cast his eyes around the room and waved a finger. 'They are listening to us now?'

Ian shook his head, resigned. 'Just the phone lines at the office.'

'As I suspected.'

'They're advisors, that's all,' Ian insisted. 'I haven't gone to the authorities – as you instructed.'

'Keep them on a short leash,' snapped van Zant. 'If I find they're getting too close, you lose the deal.'

'I don't *want* the deal!' Hart stood and ran his hand through his hair then spun away, pacing the carpet.

Van Zant watched him. 'You don't have a choice. You think this is something you can walk away from?' He shook his head. 'This is just the beginning. I'll keep squeezing until you give me what I want.'

Both men turned at a knock on the door. It opened, and Cynthia glided in.

'Oh, I'm sorry – I didn't realise we had company.'

Hart managed a smile and introduced his wife.

Van Zant stood, executed a small bow and then returned to his seat and raised a quizzical eyebrow at Hart. 'Well? What's your decision Ian?'

'I can't, Claude, you know that. My hands are tied.'

'Yours aren't the only hands tied, and you'd do well to remember that.'

Ian closed his eyes and wavered for a moment, clutching the side of the desk to steady himself. Cynthia moved towards him, but he waved her away with a frown.

'Surely we can work something out,' he said. 'A compromise?'

Claude smiled. 'I really thought Francine would have gone some way to sweeten the deal.'

'What do you mean?' Hart glanced nervously at his wife, then back at van Zant. 'What's she got to do with this?'

'She had everything to do with this,' said Claude. 'She was my gift to you.'

He stood, signalling the meeting was over.

Cynthia watched in silence as her husband almost stumbled around his desk in his haste to get the other man out of his office. As he passed her, though, the man stopped and took her hand in his, turned it over gently and kissed it.

'Madame, it was a pleasure to meet you at last. You are a formidable woman.' He smiled, then turned, nodded at Hart, and left the room.

Cynthia frowned and turned to her husband. 'Who was that?'

He sighed. 'Someone who is very pissed off that I reneged on a business deal.'

'What do you mean?'

Ian slid the photograph across the desk and turned it so Cynthia could see. 'This is what I mean.'

Cynthia cried out as she picked up the photo. 'Oh my god,' she whispered. 'Kate.'

She lowered the picture, her hands shaking, before lifting her gaze to stare at her husband.

'Ian – who the hell is Francine?'

Cynthia let the cold water run over her wrists, then splashed some onto her cheeks and forehead.

Raising her eyes to her reflection in the mirror, she tried to work out whether she appeared as sick as she felt. Dark shadows were beginning to appear under her eyes, and she swept her fingers over her forehead, trying to smooth away the worry lines which were beginning to carve a path across her skin.

She'd always suspected Ian had continued to have affairs while he was away on business, despite his past admission and promises to stop. To have his ongoing indiscretions confirmed by a total stranger had hurt her more deeply than if Ian had confessed himself.

Added to the insult was the fact that the latest affair had been a *gift* – a way to ensure a business deal went through smoothly.

She groaned, flipped down the seat of the toilet and sat with her head in her hands. Anger coursed through her body, at her husband, at her own stupidity.

Why had she waited until now to do something about Ian's affairs? Why didn't she confront him back in the States where they could each engage a lawyer and try to salvage some dignity from the whole mess?

She took a deep breath, then stood and checked her make-up in the mirror. Breathing out slowly, she set her shoulders and fluffed up her hair, before stepping towards the door and wrenched it open.

If she had her time again, would she have done anything differently?

She turned and stared at the face which reflected back at her from the mirror, and then sniffed.

Somehow, she suspected she wouldn't.

Chapter 15

The woman strode along the pavement, her hand firmly on the shoulder strap of her bag. She knew the area well, had worked there for several years, and she wasn't going to start taking chances now.

Her heels echoed off the walls of the buildings she passed, the noise from the main street fading behind her as she walked the familiar route back to the apartment. Her toes rubbed against the cheap leather of her high-heeled shoes, and she cursed as she felt a blister forming. She slowed her pace and changed her gait in an effort to ease the pain, and it was then that she heard the noise behind.

Her heart hit her ribcage hard. She quickened her step, straining her ears to hear over the *clack-clack* of her heels, cursing that she hadn't changed into her ballet flats before leaving the nightclub.

She didn't want to look back. To do so would acknowledge the danger – and slow her pace.

She cried out as her foot caught in a crack between two paving stones, and her heel rolled. The fall caught her by surprise, her elbow hitting the ground painfully as she landed, her legs curled under her body.

Gritting her teeth, she began to stand up, and then saw movement against a wall behind her, her head snapping round instantly.

'Hello, Francine.'

A smooth voice carried on the breeze towards her, before a small flame shot upwards. She recognised the man's features in the glow of the lit cigarette.

'What do you want?'

He chuckled, an eerie sound with no humour, only laced through with malice. 'You.'

Francine had no time to scream as he launched himself towards her, his hand sliding across her mouth.

The man dragged her sideways, into an alleyway off the main footpath, and then murmured into her ear. 'I need you to pass on a message for me, do you understand? Nod if you do.'

Francine nodded, her eyes wide open.

'Good, good. Now I'm going to take my hand away. Don't scream, understand?'

Francine nodded once more, and then gulped in a deep lungful of air once the man loosened his grip. Bile rose in her throat as his nicotine-stained breath warmed her face, his body odour pervasive, overpowering.

'I've done everything you asked. You've got what you wanted.'

He smiled, and Francine felt the shiver start at her blistered toes before it crawled up her spine.

'I have a message for you to pass on.' His fingers caressed her jawline, tipping her chin up until her eyes met his. 'A very special message.'

His hand shot to her mouth once more, crushing her jaw.

Francine wriggled, desperately trying to escape his grip, and then screamed into his skin as the flash of a knife cut through the air towards her.

Steve put the phone down and rubbed his eyes. Squinting in the bright early morning light which streamed between the cracks in the blinds, he picked up the documents on the small laser printer, and then turned to Finn.

'Is Hart back?'

'Yeah, he and Cynthia got in about fifteen minutes ago. The security guy who was with them said there were no incidents on the way in.'

'Okay - Hart's office. Now.'

Finn frowned and followed the other man down the corridor and through to the executive's room, closing the door behind them.

Ian looked up from his computer screen and glared at the interruption. 'What is it?'

Steve pulled out a chair and sat down, Finn following his lead.

'I've just been speaking to my contact at Interpol,' he began. 'There's no easy way to tell you this Ian, but a body was found early this morning in an alley in Aksaray. It's been confirmed that it's Francine.'

Finn watched as Hart leaned back in his chair and closed his eyes, his body crumpling.

'They're absolutely sure?' asked Ian.

'Her sister's just identified the body. She raised the alarm when she didn't return to the apartment they share last night. I'd passed on Francine's details to my contact in the hope we could speak to her, but it seems that we were too late. A road sweeper found her at dawn. She'd been left in a doorway.'

'This just keeps getting worse, doesn't it?'

'It certainly did for Francine,' murmured Finn.

Steve held up his hand to silence him, his eyes on Hart. 'When did you last see her?'

Ian leaned forward and rubbed his eyes with the heel of his hand before resting his arms on the desk. 'The night before Kate was taken. We had dinner at her place.' He paused. 'She mentioned that she'd run out of her favourite perfume and dropped a huge hint she expected me to buy her some the next day.' He sighed, folding himself back into the chair. 'That's what Kate was doing when they took her.'

Finn stirred and turned to Steve. 'What details did your contact give you?'

Steve sighed, and then spoke softly. 'She was cut. Deliberately. Everywhere. The cuts didn't kill her – the killer tormented her. The pathologist doesn't know yet how long she was alive before she was stabbed in the neck. That's what killed her – massive blood loss from the carotid artery.'

'I think I'm going to be sick.'

Hart raced from the room, and Finn heard the men's rest room door slam open in its frame before turning to Steve.

'Hope he makes it to the toilet.'

'Yeah – that hit him hard, didn't it?'

'So what else did your contact tell you?'

Steve stood and paced the room. 'The cut marks on Francine's body – the police have seen them before. A while ago, but they're too similar to discount.'

'A contract killer?'

'Mm. And someone who enjoys his work.'

'Any idea who?'

'All the signs point to a man called Yusuf.'

'Never heard of him.'

'No – you wouldn't unless you worked in this part of the world. I'm waiting for some more information to come through, but in the meantime, go and find Cynthia. I want her in the room when we speak to Ian again.'

'What's going on?' said Cynthia, as she followed her husband into the room. 'What's happened?'

'Sit down.' Finn pointed to the chairs next to Hart's desk. 'Both of you.'

He waited until they'd settled, Cynthia frowning at her husband as he dabbed a handkerchief to the corners of his mouth and then reached across his desk and pulled a glass of water towards him.

'Okay,' said Steve as they watched him expectantly. 'Listen up. We've received some information from a contact of ours, and we have a problem.'

He set out two black and white photographs on Ian's desk and pointed to the first one.

'Do either of you recognise this man?'

Cynthia frowned. 'That's the man who came to the apartment last night.'

'*What*?'

Finn looked at Steve, then back to Hart and his wife. 'You actually met him?'

Hart nodded. 'That's Claude van Zant.' His lip curled in disgust.

'What did he want? Why did he come to your apartment, not here?'

Hart shrugged. 'I think he worked out you'd stop him if he tried.'

'Too right,' said Finn, cursing the ineptness of Hart's security detail at the compound, and Hart's stupidity for not mentioning the visit sooner. 'What did he say to you?'

'That I'd have to go through with the deal. He said that Kate's life is in danger if I don't.'

Finn cursed under his breath.

'Anything else?' asked Steve.

Hart nodded and took the photograph of Kate from his pocket. 'He gave me this.'

He turned the photograph on the desk until Finn and Steve could see it.

Finn exhaled, swearing under his breath, and noticed that Cynthia's face had paled.

'But you knew he was dangerous, didn't you Hart?'

Hart shook his head. 'Not at first, no.' He glanced at Cynthia. 'That's the truth, I swear.' He rubbed the back of his neck before continuing. 'When he approached me six months ago, he introduced himself as van Zant and said he represented a small organisation in the Mediterranean who are interested in the system I'd been working on for the Turkish military.'

'Who is he really?' asked Cynthia, taking the photograph from her husband and frowning.

'Yusuf,' said Steve. 'Possibly more dangerous than his boss. He's the henchman for the organisation. Does all the wet work.'

'Wet work?' said Cynthia, her brow creasing.

'The killing. Probably killed Francine.' Finn paused and glared at Ian. 'And he's the one who has Kate.'

Cynthia put her hand to her mouth and slowly shook her head. 'I can't believe this is happening.'

'They must want the parts badly,' Steve said to Finn, then turned back to Hart and shrugged. 'Most people who meet Yusuf don't survive long.'

Hart shivered. 'I had no idea.'

Steve pointed to the second photograph.

'What about this man? Have either of you met him?'

The picture showed a man in his late teens with jet-black hair leaning against an old army vehicle, a rifle slung over his arms. The picture had been taken while the vehicle had been parked under the shade of trees, the dappled light casting shadows across the man's face.

'I don't know this man.'

Finn pushed the photograph to one side and placed a photocopy of a newspaper clipping on the desk, a grainy photograph of a man walking through a train station concourse set next to a short report about a car bombing in the 1980s.

'And this man?'

Hart frowned. 'I'm not sure – he's changed his appearance here, hasn't he?'

Finn looked over his shoulder at Steve, who nodded.

'It's a few years older. It's estimated he was in his mid-twenties when this was taken nearly thirty years ago. No-one's got a photograph of him since – he's been extremely careful. We think he may have had more plastic surgery since then, particularly the nose,' he said.

'Do you know his name?' asked Cynthia.

'It's Kaan. We think he's Yusuf's current employer.'

'Who is he?' asked Cynthia. 'I mean, how bad is this?'

'No-one knows his real name,' said Steve. 'Kaan seems to be as close as anyone's going to get based on the intel available. Some say he's Syrian, others that he's Kurdish. Most of our contacts believe him to be using the Kurdish rebel cause as an excuse to start his own battle with the Westernised end of the Mediterranean.'

He passed a folder of newspaper cuttings and intelligence reports to Finn who began to flick through them. 'I'm amazed we have *any* photographs of him.'

'He sees himself as a freedom fighter,' said Steve, 'so at first he wasn't adverse to a bit of publicity for his cause.' He pointed at the newspaper clipping in Finn's hand. 'That's the last known photograph of him – taken thirty years ago.'

Cynthia turned to her husband, tapping the edge of the photograph with a manicured nail. 'Why can't you just give him what he wants? Sign the deal.'

'I can't, not now that I know he lied about who he was. I originally thought he was from another department in the Turkish military. If I sold him the parts now, it'd contravene EU and UN sanctions on what components can be sold for weaponry outside of approved government contracts. The fact that I know van Zant, or Yusuf – whatever he's called – will use it to finish building a weapon which is banned, and that he'll probably use it – I just can't. It'll destroy the business, and I'll end up in prison.'

'I can't believe you put Kate's life on the line for a quick tumble in the sheets and a business deal!' snapped Cynthia. She stood and walked towards the door, jerking it open. 'You're pathetic.'

Finn and Steve remained silent after the door slammed behind her. Hart managed to appear contrite before turning to the two men.

'What do we do now?'

'There's that 'we' again,' murmured Finn.

Chapter 16

Finn looked over his shoulder as the door opened, and Steve walked in, followed by an older man of medium height, black hair shot with grey clipped close to his scalp, and keen brown eyes.

He wore a tan coloured suit, polished brown shoes, and a frown across his face.

'Gents, this is Emrah Ahmed, Turkish Military Intelligence,' said Steve.

'Hang on,' said Hart. 'I thought we weren't involving the police?' He turned to Steve. 'Why wasn't I consulted on this?'

Emrah crossed the room, pulled out a chair and sat down, leaned forward and glared at Hart.

'Sir, you lost the right to be consulted the moment you chose not to alert us to the fact you have been communicating with a known terrorist.'

'Emrah has been assigned to the case. My contact with Interpol has managed to persuade the Turkish authorities to allow us to work with them,' explained Steve.

'You had better bring me up to speed,' said Emrah. 'Quickly.'

After listening to Finn and Steve run through the facts, Emrah held up his hand.

'How are you going to persuade him to hand over the woman?'

'It's clear we're dealing with a complex personality,' said Steve. 'Kaan is highly educated, very intelligent and probably very charming when he wants to be.'

'Or when he wants something,' said Hart.

Steve nodded. 'He's probably been planning this for a long time. Doing his homework on the business, waiting for an opportunity to use you.' He turned the page of the report he'd been sent. 'The problem we have,' he said, 'is that someone with this sort of personality has no morals. Which puts Kate's life at risk if we don't do what Kaan wants.'

'What do you mean?' asked Hart.

'What he means,' said Finn, 'is even if we hand over the parts, Kaan will kill Kate.'

He stopped pacing, crossed his arms across his chest and stared at Hart. 'We have to come up with a way to rescue her, while Kaan thinks we're still negotiating.'

Emrah coughed. 'I'm sorry gentlemen, but what makes you think *you* will be conducting any rescue?'

Finn frowned, and then pointed at himself and Steve. 'Because that's what we do.'

'You are on Turkish soil. And *I* am running this investigation.'

'With all due respect,' said Steve, holding up a hand to interrupt Finn's protests, 'we've already made a hell of a lot of progress before I called you. Finn's been working all hours tracing leads and following them up.' He pulled up a chair opposite the intelligence officer. 'Not only that, but she's an American citizen, not Turkish.' He leaned back and pointed at Finn. 'Having an ex-FBI hostage expert involved in the search for one of their own? That's got to count for something, right?'

'Not only that,' said Finn, 'My specialisation is hostage rescue. Not negotiation – *rescue*.'

Emrah snorted, and then looked at Steve. 'This is the man who fell to pieces three years ago and is only here today because you were his babysitter, isn't that right?'

Steve left his seat the moment he saw Finn move. Before he could reach the intelligence officer, Steve had him in an arm lock against the office wall.

'Now is *not* the time,' he hissed in Finn's ear and let go.

Finn exhaled, turned his back on Emrah and walked to the middle of the room, his hands on his hips.

Steve checked he wasn't going to have second thoughts, and then sat back down. 'That was uncalled for, and you know it.'

Emrah raised his hands to placate Finn. 'It was, I apologise.' He turned back to Steve. 'But you see my point? He is unpredictable.'

'You provoked him,' said Steve. 'I've been working with this man for a long time. I'd trust him with my life – and have. If we're going to have any success in finding Kate alive and well, then rescuing her, I want Finn on board.' He raised an eyebrow at Emrah. 'Well?'

The intelligence officer balled his hand into a fist and tapped it on the arm of the chair, assessing each of the men in front of him.

'Alright. But you report to me at all times, is that clear?'

Both men nodded.

'Alright,' said Emrah and stood to leave. 'I will begin to mobilise a team of investigators and review what you've found out so far.' He checked his watch. 'I will telephone you in three hours for an update.'

Steve showed him to the door, then closed it and turned to face the room.

'Okay,' said Finn, approaching Hart's desk, 'now we've got that out of the way, how are we going to deal with this?'

Hart took a handkerchief from his pocket and dabbed his forehead. 'If we give those parts to Kaan, it'll be the tipping point for this part of the world,' he said. 'It'll be the last thing needed to tear apart the Middle East and this side of the Mediterranean.'

'What about fitting the parts with a tracking device?' Finn suggested. 'At least then, we'll be able to follow him.'

'There's no room,' said Hart. 'Each part is a sealed metal cylinder. The guts of it are made up of micro-processors, specifically designed to fit the cylinder. We designed it that way so no modifications were needed to the existing missile system the army is currently using.'

'What's the status of the parts?' asked Finn.

'They're in the final testing stage at our research and development laboratory in Nevada. The shipment was due to be made at the end of next week.'

'How big are they?'

Hart held his middle finger and thumb apart. 'About eight centimetres. There are two of them – the mechanics are encased in metal cylinders to stop grease and dirt getting caught up in the electronics. You could hold both cylinders in your hand.'

Finn picked up the phone and placed it in front of Hart. 'Phone them. Tell them to halt the testing and get the parts shipped here now.'

'But they're not ready!'

'I don't care – and Kaan doesn't know they're not ready. Just get them here.'

Finn spent the next hour coaching Hart through what he would have to do and say when Yusuf next telephoned with demands.

'For Christ's sake remember you don't know his real name,' said Finn. 'To you, he's still Claude van Zant.'

Hart nodded. 'I understand.'

'Good. Now, when he asks if you're going to hand over the parts, don't sound too eager, but don't give him time to add to his demands either,' said Finn. 'You can tell him that you're going to give in and give them to him but make sure he understands you're having to get them from the testing facility in the States. Get as much time as you can to do that, understand?'

Hart nodded, a picture of misery. 'What's he going to do when he finds out they won't work?'

Finn shrugged. 'With any luck, by the time he finds that out, it'll be the least of his problems.'

Now, the three men were in Hart's office, their patience tested while they waited for van Zant's call.

Hart paced the carpet behind his desk, unable to sit still while Finn slumped in an armchair, his foot tapping the floor.

He'd closed his eyes, willing his heartbeat to slow down, but still heard the blood rushing in his ears, while adrenalin coursed his veins.

He opened one eye and saw Steve lying on a sofa he'd dragged into the office from the hallway. He had his arms behind his head, eyes closed. Finn envied the man's outward calmness.

Then the telephone rang, and the men lunged into action.

Hart waited until Steve had the headphones over his ears and gave him the thumbs up before answering.

'Hello?'

'Mr Hart, good afternoon.'

'I don't have time for pleasantries, van Zant. What do you want?'

'Very well. What is your decision in relation to the parts I want?'

Ian sighed. 'You really don't leave me a lot of choice, do you?' he said.

'So you will procure them for me?'

'It's not a case of *procuring* them,' said Hart, and raised his head to see Finn wink at him. 'They're prototypes. They're not easily obtained.'

'I'm on a very tight schedule, Mr Hart,' said van Zant, his voice lowering. 'So I must insist that you obtain the parts for me as soon as possible.'

'I'll need at least forty-eight hours,' said Hart. 'I have to contact my testing facility, arrange for the parts to be packaged correctly, shipped here, and then checked through Customs. It's not going to be easy.'

A silence permeated the telephone line, and Hart looked up and frowned at Steve, who shook his head.

'You will have thirty-six hours to get the parts to Istanbul,' came the reply. 'I will contact you again then.'

The phone went dead, and the men slid the headphones off as Hart put down the receiver.

'Well,' said Finn. 'Thirty-six hours is better than twenty-four, I suppose.'

Chapter 17

The door burst open, and the two kidnappers strode across the room towards Kate, took hold of an arm each and hauled her to her feet.

'What's going on? Where are you taking me?' she demanded and tried to pull away from them.

'You'll soon see,' replied the older man, a malicious grin on his face. He held up the hood and whipped it over her head before she had time to react.

Her wrist was lifted, and the metal clasp unhinged. She desperately wanted to rub the soreness around her bones, but then both wrists were grabbed, and she felt the familiar rope bind them together.

'Walk.'

Kate allowed herself to be led from the room and along the passageway towards the stairs. She found that if she closed her eyes, she could concentrate and get her bearings. If she opened her eyes and saw the hessian material of the hood, she panicked, memories flooding her mind. Eyes closed, she could focus and build upon the map she'd created in her mind of her surroundings.

The two men led her down the two flights of stairs and into the room where she'd first met Kaan yesterday.

Was it only yesterday? She mentally checked the day marks in her head. Surely he didn't need more proof of life?

She began to hyperventilate, visualising what might lie in wait for her, and then gasped as she was forced down into a sitting position. Luckily her backside found the chair, but she wobbled and felt her heart lurch in her chest. Someone grabbed her shoulder to steady her, and she felt balanced enough to place her bound hands in her lap.

'Thank you,' she murmured.

The hood was torn from her head, and she sucked in her breath as a few strands of hair went with it. She blinked in the sudden light streaming down onto her from dirty windows which surrounded one side of the room.

Ignoring the man sat in front of her, she concentrated on the sounds she could hear in the background. Men shouting to one another, as if they were in a hurry, busy.

The man in front of her clicked his fingers in her face.

'Concentrate Miss Foster,' he said. 'You're going to do something for me.' He smiled, and Kate's blood ran cold.

'What?'

He pointed to a small video camera mounted on a tripod to his right.

Kate's stomach tumbled, and her insides quivered. *Surely not*. She looked from the camera to Kaan and back again. Surely they weren't going to execute her?

The man obviously read her thoughts, and began to chuckle.

'Fear not, Miss Foster,' he said. 'We are not the barbarians you imagine. Your life is not in danger. For today, at least.' He shrugged.

Kate tilted her head back and breathed out. To hell with it, if the man saw she was relieved, she didn't care. Her mind raced, though. What did he mean about 'for today'?

'What do you want from me this time?'

In response, he pushed a piece of A4-sized paper towards her. On it, in large capital letters, a message had been scrawled out.

'No way.' Kate read the message and stared at Kaan. 'Absolutely not.'

She heard the slap before she felt it. The man moved across the desk so fast, she had no time to react.

Her head whipped round to the right, and the muscles in her neck constricted. Her cheek stung with the blow, and her eyes and nose began to water. Tears of shock and pain ran down her face.

By the time she'd turned back to Kaan, he'd already sat back in his chair, unflustered. He waited until her sobs had subsided, and then leaned forward. 'You *will*.'

He looked over her head and nodded.

One of the kidnappers walked across to the camera and began checking the settings. Kate baulked as the other kidnapper dragged the chair, with her still on it, so that it was away from the desk and in clear view of the camera's lens.

He turned, picked up the piece of paper from where it lay on the desk and moved behind the camera, facing her.

'Do you require reading glasses?' asked Kaan.

Kate shook her head. Her bottom lip trembled, and she brought her bound hands to her face to wipe the tears away. She sniffed, and then took a deep breath. If she was going to have to do this, then she had better make sure she was damn coherent. She didn't expect to get a second chance.

'Begin.' Kaan's calm voice resonated around the room, and for a moment Kate wondered why he didn't record his own message.

Then she realised. Maybe no-one knew his face.

Clever.

The red light on the front of the camera began to flash, and the man operating it nodded at her once.

She took another deep breath, and then began to recite the words Kaan had written.

'My name is Kate Foster. I am an American citizen, and I am currently a prisoner of Kaan…'

Forty seconds later, it was done.

Kate dropped her head the moment the red light on the camera stopped flashing and closed her eyes.

She opened her eyes at the sound of Kaan clapping next to her.

'Well done,' he said. 'You see, it wasn't so hard.' He flicked his hand at the two men. 'Take her back.'

Kate was hauled to her feet and the hood placed over her head once more.

As she was led from the room, she listened – Kaan was still talking to one of the kidnappers. She shuffled her feet and slowed down, straining her ears.

'Wait.'

The man guiding Kate towards the stairs stopped. His fingers dug into her arm as he turned back to the room.

'If we don't get a satisfactory response within the timeframe we've given them, prepare to move her,' said Kaan. 'No traces.'

Kate was jerked towards the staircase, her mind racing as she climbed. Reaching her room, the hood was removed and her hands untied before her wrist was encased within the metal clasp once more.

As the door shut, Finn's last words to her resonated in her mind.

If they move you, they're going to kill you.

Kate walked to the window and let her gaze fall to the day marks.

She was running out of time.

Hart put down the phone.

'There's a package at reception I have to collect,' he said.

Finn caught Steve's expression and shook his head. 'You don't collect anything,' he said. 'I'll go.'

He hurried from the room and ran to the internal stairs rather than wait for the elevator. He swung round the last newel post and burst through the door into the lobby, where the receptionist jumped in her seat at his entrance.

'Package for Ian Hart?'

She pointed to the reception desk. 'There.'

Finn walked over to her. The package was rectangular in shape, covered in brown paper, with Hart's name scrawled across the front in black permanent marker.

To the alarm of the receptionist, Finn pulled a pair of gloves from his pocket.

'Have you touched this?'

She nodded.

'Show me where – just point. Don't touch it again.'

She did as he instructed.

'Okay, good. That's not too bad.' Finn leaned over the counter and took a pair of scissors from the desk tidy. He carefully snipped open the packaging and peered inside.

His heart stopped.

'When was this dropped off?' he said. 'The exact time.'

'I don't know – sorry. I'd gone to the bathroom. When I came back, it was on the desk there.'

Finn looked around the room until he saw the security camera which faced the desk and the front door. With any luck, they'd have the courier on record, and would be able to give the image to Emrah.

He picked up the package and raced back up the stairs. As he entered Hart's office, he held up the USB stick in his gloved hand.

'I'm presuming your laptop has a multi-media player?'

'Yes.'

Finn passed the packaging to Steve, who had already donned gloves. 'Best get this across to Emrah as soon as possible.'

'Let's see what's on the stick first, and then we can let him have a copy of it as well.'

'Check the security camera too,' said Finn.

'Will do.'

Finn moved round to where Hart sat. 'Move.'

Hart shot out of his chair and stood to one side, hovering.

Finn sat down, pulled the chair closer to the desk. He closed his eyes. 'Password?'

No answer.

'Password?' Finn repeated and looked over his shoulder.

Hart had gone bright red. 'Francine,' he mumbled.

'Jesus.' Finn shook his head and typed in the letters.

Once he'd accessed the desktop, he located the media player software and inserted the USB stick into the side of the laptop.

Finn adjusted the volume, and then clicked the 'play' button.

The recording began, and he clenched his fist at the sight of Kate brushing her cheeks. She'd obviously been crying, and he exhaled sharply at the sight of the red welt across one side of her face.

She began speaking, shakily at first, then her voice growing steady. Her eyes were focused to one side of the lens, and Finn realised that she was reading from a prepared script.

'You will phone this number when the parts are ready to be dropped off.'

Finn reached over the desk and scribbled down the number she recited and passed it to Steve, before turning back to the recording. He ignored the sound of Steve leaving the room, his entire focus on Kate.

'Any attempt...' she began, and then broke off, stifling a sob.

Finn's heart twisted. He knew what was coming.

Kate began again. 'Any attempt to trace the parts, rescue me or track down my location will result in my immediate death.'

Her body began to shake, one heel bouncing off the floor with nerves, and Finn saw how she set her shoulders before completing the message.

'If you fail in your duties, and the parts are not received by the deadline, I will die.'

She fell silent and Finn counted the seconds before the camera was switched off, Kate's eyes boring into his.

Ignoring Hart's questions, he replayed the recording three times before copying it to another USB stick.

Pocketing both, he turned from the computer and walked to the command post. Closing the door behind him, he approached Steve, who was putting a copy of the security tape from the reception area into a padded envelope.

Steve turned as Finn approached, and dropped the package onto the desk before placing his hand on Finn's arm.

'That bad?'

Finn nodded. 'Yeah. Give me a few seconds.'

He collapsed into a chair and held his head in his hands. Closing his eyes, he forced himself to calm down. Anger wouldn't help get him through this. He had to focus. Plan. Execute the plan. He breathed out, and opened his eyes.

'Okay, how did you get on with the security camera footage?'

'They used a kid.'

'A kid?'

'Yeah, watch.' Steve played the recording from the security tape and then paused it as a thin teenager in jeans and an old t-shirt walked into the frame.

'Have we got a face?'

The other man nodded, and ran the recording. When the boy turned from the reception desk, he looked up – straight into the lens of the camera.

'Can you get me an image capture of that?'

'Sure can. What are you thinking?'

'Just a hunch at the moment. Hold on.' Finn pulled his mobile phone out of his pocket, scrolled through the contacts list, and then hit the 'call' button.

The call connected after only three rings.

'Mr Kadír? Finn Scott here. I've got a photo of someone we think might be connected to the kidnapping we're investigating. If I email it to you, could you ask Osman to look at it straight away and call me back?'

Finn wrote down the shopkeeper's email address, and then disconnected the call.

While Steve uploaded the photograph and sent the message, Finn sat down, tapping his foot on the floor, and stared at his phone, willing the shopkeeper's son to confirm his hunch.

'You think the garage owner would use his own son as a courier?' said Steve, turning in his chair.

Finn shrugged. 'Sometimes it's the simplest connection, isn't it? I mean, we might be dealing with threats from one of the most dangerous people in this part of the world, but it doesn't mean the people he employs are as clever or ruthless.'

'They've got some nerve.'

'It's either arrogance or stupidity, I'm not sure which.'

Finn scratched the stubble which had formed on his chin. 'I suspect the latter.'

The phone rang, and he almost dropped it. Glancing across at Steve, he checked the incoming called ID then answered it.

'Mr Kadír.' Finn ran a hand over his face as he listened, his heart pounding against his ribs. 'Okay, that's great – and thank your son for me, will you?'

He disconnected the call. 'Kadír's son just confirmed the boy in the photograph is his school friend, Halim,' he said.

Steve exhaled, leaned back and stared at the ceiling.

Finn stood and slapped him on the shoulder. 'Okay, we just caught a break. Let's not waste it.'

Steve nodded, leaned forward and began to gather together the security tapes. 'I'll get these off to Emrah – did you do a copy of the recording?'

Finn handed both copies to him.

'If it's okay with you, I'm going to watch it now.'

'Go for it. Apart from grabbing the phone number she recited, that's all I had.' Finn said, and watched as Steve inserted the stick into his own laptop. 'The room she's in has windows – there's light on her face – but there's no indication of where she might be.'

'Okay, let's have a look.'

Finn sat with his chin in his hands as the recording played in front of his eyes once more. He frowned when Steve replayed the last ten seconds when Kate had started to shake.

Steve spun round to face him with a grin on his face. 'Clever girl.'

'What?'

'You didn't see it?'

'No – what?'

'She sent you a message. Watch.'

Finn chewed a nail as Steve rewound the recording once more. *What had he seen?*

He shook his head. 'Enough games. We're running out of time. What message did you see?'

Steve smiled, replayed the tape and pointed to Kate's knee as it bobbed up and down.

'Tell me the one person you know who has the annoying habit of doing this when he's wound up.'

Me.

Finn frowned, and then began to smile as the last few seconds played out.

'She never told me she knew Morse code.'

Unknown to Kaan, Kate had just sent a message to the two hostage specialists.

Car. Garage. Space.

Chapter 18

The garage owner pushed the boy away from the bench and cuffed the side of his head as he passed.

'Keep him away from us,' growled Yusuf. 'He's too nosy.'

'I am sorry, Yusuf – he is a schoolboy – he wants to learn about everything.'

The younger man frowned.

'What is that around your neck?'

Mustafa grinned, fingering Kate's necklace.

'The woman's – she was flaunting it in front of me. It is a fine piece, is it not?'

'Yes, it is,' said Yusuf, and then moved forwards and tore it from the man's neck. 'You are an idiot! Did you not think someone might see you wearing this?'

'I – I...'

'Enough.' Yusuf pushed the necklace into his shirt pocket. 'Go – and keep an eye on your boy. Leave us.'

He watched as the older man turned and tried to ignore the weight of the woman's necklace, the thin fabric of his shirt doing little to prevent it rubbing against his skin.

Kate let her head drop forward, closed her eyes and tried to ignore the sweat running between her breasts and seeping into her bra. In the distance, a car horn blared once, closely followed by another. The sun had peaked over the building some time ago and the afternoon air was lethargic, heavy with the smell of spices.

She hadn't seen Halim today. The old man had brought her food and water instead, taking great delight in removing her necklace from within the folds of his shirt and holding it up, letting it spin in the air.

Kate had ignored the gesture. She'd seen the mess the man's fist had made of Halim's cheek, and she had no desire to give the man a chance to hit her – or worse. She shivered.

At the back of her mind, Finn's voice kept reminding her that she was now in mortal danger. She'd never forgotten his last words to her after the training weekend. They were etched in her mind and, if she was honest with herself, had been the entire time she'd been working overseas.

Her head suddenly shot up. A memory – something about looking for opportunities, however small they seemed. Finn's words echoed in her head. She frowned, and then shuffled forward to peer at the wall to which she'd been shackled.

Her fingers traced the chain which connected the metal clasp around her wrist to an iron loop fixed to the wall. She tugged at the chain, tentatively at first, then harder. It rattled, but the links remained locked together, unyielding. Kate's hands moved to her wrist, felt around the clasp which bound it and turned it so that the hinges faced her. The smooth outside surface protected the locking mechanism. She cursed in frustration, slapped the metal surface, and fell back to the floor, exasperated.

As she sat, her eyes caught a motion on the wall. She held her breath, and then tugged hard at the chain once more. A faint smile began to form on her lips. Although the chain held tight, the metal loop in the wall moved slightly in the mortar. She dropped the chain and moved across the floor to the wall to inspect it more closely.

Kneeling, she rubbed her finger against the pale coloured mortar and was rewarded with a small cloud of dust which tumbled to the floor. Glancing over her shoulder towards the door, she repeated the process, and managed to dislodge a little more. Her smile broadened, until she peered down and noticed the cement dust which now covered the floor by her knees.

She swore, pushed herself upright and glared at the crumbs on the floor. Exhaling heavily, she tried to ignore her heart pounding between her ribs. She stepped back from the wall, then tripped over her bedding and fell onto the concrete floor. She cried out in frustration and untangled the bedding from her feet.

As she pushed it out of her way, an idea formed. Scrambling to her feet she pushed the mattress until it was flush against the wall, and then tossed the coverings back onto it.

The mortar dust now hidden, she sat down and inspected the cuts to her fingers where she'd attacked the mortar.

She peered at the metal hoop protruding from the walls and then back to the bloodied tips of her fingers. It was no good – she'd have to find some sort of tool to use, otherwise she would never loosen the iron fittings.

She gathered up the chain so it wouldn't make a noise as she walked backwards and forwards across the room, her eyes scanning the floor.

She worked on the premise that the room had been prepared in a hurry, evidenced by the slipshod paint job on the window panes, and that there might be something lying around that she could put to use.

She worked a section of the floor at a time, resting her ankle between each. She listened to the noises in the building, ready to return to her mattress and feign innocence the moment she heard footsteps.

Luck was on her side. On her third search of the room, in the far corner beyond the door, she found what she had been looking for.

A nail, bent and rusted, had avoided being swept up by whoever had prepared the room. She stretched the chain as far as it would reach and ignored the metal clasp as it dug into the skin around her wrist as she strained her fingers towards the crude tool.

She knelt down and picked it up, a broad grin across her face, and then she scurried back to her mattress and began to scrape at the dry mortar.

Kate began on the side of the hoop which was furthest from the door, working on the premise that her handiwork wouldn't be seen easily by someone entering the room.

Using the nail, she quickly dislodged a large chunk of the wall and kicked the dust under the mattress. She was so engrossed in her work that she didn't hear the approach of footsteps.

Her head shot round at the sound of the bolts being drawn back from the door. She quickly pushed the nail under the mattress and sat down, her back against the wall and forced herself to calm her breathing.

She rubbed at her ankle to give herself something to focus on when Yusuf entered the room, a small bowl of stew in one hand and a fresh bottle of water in the other.

She ignored him while he set down the items in front of her, turning her head when she caught him leering at her, dreading to think what Kaan would let the man do to her once he decided she was no longer of any use to him.

She shuddered and then cursed inwardly. Yusuf had noticed her reaction and glared at her.

His eyes shifted from the door to where she sat. He seemed agitated, his movements nervous. He licked his lips as he stood, and then he stared down at her and moved his gun from shoulder to shoulder. As he moved, the scent of his sweat and unwashed body wafted across Kate, and she turned her head away.

Yusuf moved quickly, crouched down and grabbed her jaw in his fist.

'Don't stare at me like that.' His lip curled, his eyes blazing.

'I'm sorry,' Kate whispered.

His eyes glazed, and Kate noticed the fresh pinprick on the inside of his arm. His breath, sweet and sickly, brushed her forehead.

Kate kept her gaze on him, terrified of what he would do to her if she dared to turn away.

His fingers moved down her jaw, then encircled her neck. He jerked her hard towards him, and she put up her hands, pressing against the stained cotton of his t-shirt and straining against him.

Grease and sweat clung to her fingers, and she whimpered, feeling his hardness pressing against her.

A door slammed on the floor beneath them, and a voice carried up the stairs.

'Yusuf! We need you down here!'

The man stepped away from her and sneered. 'When we leave here, I shall claim you as my prize from Kaan,' he said. 'You will do well to fear me, woman.'

Kate closed her eyes, and then cried out as he released her, pushing her back against the wall, before he turned and left the room, cursing under his breath.

Kate waited until the door swung shut and the bolts shot back into place, and then slid her back down the wall until she was in a crouching position. She shuffled round on her feet and counted slowly to one hundred. Downstairs, she heard the low murmur of voices before a door slammed again and the building fell silent.

She finished counting, then lifted the thin mattress and extracted the rusted nail.

Moving into a crouching position, she began digging into the mortar once more.

She had no idea what Hart was doing to rescue her, but she suspected she was rapidly running out of time.

'The only person who's going to get you out of here is you,' she whispered. 'So you'd better get a move on, Kate Foster.'

Chapter 19

A brief knock on the door preceded the receptionist walking into the office.

'Mr Hart, the package from the States has just arrived in reception.'

'Thanks.' Hart turned to Finn as the woman left the room. 'This is it then, isn't it?'

'It looks that way.'

Steve walked across the room and held out Ian's mobile phone to him. 'Phone the number Kate read out in her video,' he said, handing Hart a slip of paper. 'Keep the conversation short, and again, buy us as much time as possible.'

Finn checked his watch. 'We're well ahead of schedule. Suggest to him you need to check the parts, make sure they weren't damaged during transit or something.' He turned to Steve. 'We need to aim for late tomorrow for the exchange if we can.'

'Why?' asked Ian, frowning.

'People clock off work earlier for the weekend. It'll be quiet so we can recce any drop-off point,' said Finn.

Steve nodded. 'He's right. Are you ready?'

Hart exhaled loudly and turned his eyes towards the ceiling. 'Yes.' He looked at both of the men. 'Yes, I guess I am.'

He took the phone from Steve and dialled the number, turning his back on the men, who hurried over to the communications equipment and slipped headphones over their ears.

'Sounds like it's being pinged off another exchange,' said Finn.

Steve shook his head and frowned, placing a finger on his lips.

After three rings, the phone was answered.

'Speak.'

'The parts have arrived.'

'Good. They are ready?'

'I – um, no. Not quite.' Hart ran his hand over his forehead, a bead of sweat running down his temple.

'What do you mean?'

Hart took a deep breath. 'I need to check them – run some tests.' He turned to Steve, who nodded. 'The packaging is damaged. I want to make sure the parts are okay.'

'How long will that take?'

Finn held his hands apart and pulled them away from each other.

Hart frowned, and then nodded, understanding. 'I can't say. At least twenty-four hours, I should think. I'll need to get one of my engineers here to help me, and we'll be working through the night running diagnostics. If they are damaged, we'll need to fix them.'

Finn mimed clapping his hands.

Hart frowned at him, and then turned his back again.

'That is over the allocated time.'

Hart inhaled sharply. 'It is, I know, I'm sorry – but the parts *have* arrived earlier than we anticipated, haven't they?'

The silence stretched along the phone line.

Finn pushed the headphones closer to his ears, trying to ignore the sound of his heartbeat in his ears and listen through the slight hiss of static.

'You have until six tomorrow night.'

Hart spun on his heel.

Finn punched the air and nodded.

Hart tipped his head back and closed his eyes, before calming his voice. 'Okay, yes. I can work to that. Where do you want me to bring them?'

'I will phone you on this number with further instructions two hours before the drop-off time. Do not lose this phone, Mr Hart. It is your only lifeline to Miss Foster.'

Finn pushed his sunglasses up his nose and leaned forward, his hand gripping the steering wheel, his jaw clenched.

Steve's mobile phone vibrated on the dashboard, making both men start in their seats, before Steve answered it.

Ending the call, he turned to Finn. 'Grab team's in place,' he said. 'The school's about to turn out for the day.'

Finn exhaled and started the car. 'About time.'

He left the engine running and drummed his fingers on the steering wheel. 'They're sure the target will take this route?'

'They followed him yesterday as soon as I told Emrah we suspected him. Best they can do.'

Finn adjusted the rear view mirror, and then looked up when Steve nudged his arm.

'Here we go.'

A man and a boy were walking along the road towards them.

Finn frowned. If the boy was meant to be the same age as Osman Kadír, then he was small for a thirteen-year-old.

Halim shuffled along the pavement beside his father, his shoulders slumped, hands in the pockets of his school uniform trousers.

The garage owner had been identified earlier that day by Emrah's team as Mustafa Rizman. He had been easily traced, having been implicated in a car theft racket five years earlier, where he'd been released on probation due to lack of concrete evidence.

The man was talking to the boy, hands animated while he spoke to his son. At one point, he slapped Halim behind the head, the teenager ducking out of range of a second blow. The man continued to gesticulate, while the boy continued to walk alongside him, his eyes to the ground.

'Happy family,' murmured Steve.

'What happens to the boy?'

'Emrah will get child services to sit in with him while he's interviewed.'

'And after that, when we charge his dad with assisting a terrorist?'

'Don't think about it. I expect they've got a good social care system which will care for him.'

As the couple drew closer, Finn's heart began to beat rapidly. If Emrah's team didn't time the take-down right, all their plans were going to go south – and fast.

'How long do you think it'll be before they miss him?'

'I don't know. Couple of hours?'

'It's his business – do you think they'll believe he's done a runner?'

Steve sighed. 'The man's not the brightest bad guy I've known,' he said. 'I'm hoping they'll think he's got cold feet. Taken his son away from the danger.'

Finn tensed as a black SUV rounded the corner at the end of the road behind Mustafa and Halim.

The vehicle crawled along the road, the driver waiting until there was space to pull alongside the two pedestrians, and then picked up speed.

Finn floored the accelerator and swung the car out of its parking space. He drove straight at the man and his boy, sliding to a stop when the car mounted the pavement in front of them.

In seconds, the SUV was alongside, its side door ripped open and a team of four masked men jumped out and surrounded Mustafa and Halim.

'Move,' their leader said.

Finn swallowed as Halim stared at his father, his face pitiful.

'Shit, I hate this part.'
'Me too.'

One of the masked men took Halim by the hand and led him into the vehicle. The boy went meekly, glancing once over his shoulder at his father who was struggling with the three remaining men.

As the leader drew out a syringe, Halim's captor turned his head and gently pushed the teenager into the vehicle.

Mustafa slumped to the pavement with the effects of the tranquiliser, his legs buckling under him.

At a signal from the leader, the remaining two men hauled Mustafa into the SUV and the vehicle sped away.

Finn checked his watch. 'Fifteen seconds.'

'They're good.'

'Hate to think how they get the practice.'

Finn sighed, slipped the car into gear and reversed off the pavement before turning and steering the car in the direction taken by the SUV.

'Okay, let's see what we've got.'

Emrah led the way along a dimly-lit corridor, the pale green walls casting a sickly glow in the innards of the police station.

After dropping Steve at Hart's offices, Finn had sped to the intelligence officer's temporary base.

'You can have five minutes with him,' said Emrah over his shoulder. 'My boss will have a heart attack if he finds out an American was interviewing a Turkish suspect.'

Finn clenched his fists as he followed the man towards the interview room. 'Five minutes is fine,' he lied. 'We appreciate it.'

Emrah nodded, mollified for the present time. 'I will be in the room as well.'

Finn shrugged. 'No problem – I don't speak Turkish anyway.'

The intelligence officer turned, raised an eyebrow and leaned against the door to the interview room.

'Ready?'

'Can we take a look first?

Emrah nodded, stepped to one side and pulled a cord. A section of material moved along the wall, revealing a window to the cell.

'He can't see us.'

Finn stared through the glass at Mustafa who was sitting, handcuffed to a simple wooden table, a wad of cloth held to a cut on his cheek.

A plastic bottle of water had been placed on the table, its contents half drained.

The man's brown eyes lifted to the mirror in the room and he scowled.

'Friendly sort.'

'Indeed. Are you ready now?'

Finn straightened. 'Let's get on with it.'

He followed Emrah into the room and instantly recoiled at the foul air.

The Turkish intelligence officer shrugged. 'An unfortunate side effect of the tranquiliser,' he murmured and indicated that Finn should take one of the chairs opposite Mustafa.

As he sat, Finn's eyes roamed the array of plastic bags which had been laid out on the table, out of reach of the handcuffed prisoner.

'Gloves?'

Emrah reached into his jacket pocket and retrieved two pairs, handing one set to Finn.

He put them on, and then reached across and began sifting through the small collection, mentally committing the contents to memory.

A packet of cigarettes, a set of keys, a wallet.

Finn stared across the table at Mustafa.

The man was sweating, his eyes following the path of Finn's hand.

Emrah coughed next to him. 'Three minutes.'

Finn ignored him and watched Mustafa's reaction as he moved his hand over the bag containing the man's mobile phone.

His shoulders slumped, and he sat back in his chair, dabbing at his cheek with the cloth.

Finn pulled the zip lock bag across the table and took out the phone, then activated it.

'Pin code?'

The man pouted. 'Two, six, six, nine.'

Finn began scrolling through the contacts list. Empty. He switched to the recent calls and started again.

'One minute, Mr Scott.'

He held up his hand to silence Emrah, and then blinked.

He thumbed back up the list and re-read the number in front of him, then pushed the chair back.

'Outside – now,' he said.

Emrah unlocked the door and both men stepped into the corridor.

Finn waited until the door was shut, then held up the mobile phone.

'I need you to buy me some time.'

The intelligence officer frowned and crossed his arms across his chest. 'Explain.'

Finn told him.

'I see.' He held out his hand for the phone. 'I can give you two hours – no more.'

'Thanks.'

Finn slapped him on the shoulder and hurried away. As he walked down the steps of the police station and into the cool air of the late afternoon, he took out his own mobile phone.

'Steve? We've got a problem. I need you to do something for me.'

Chapter 20

Finn approached the boardroom table, pulled out a photograph showing the plastic evidence bag containing Mustafa Rizman's mobile phone and threw it onto the polished surface.

It skidded across, stopping when it hit Cynthia's elbow.

She closed her eyes.

'Care to tell me why your mobile phone number is in a terrorist's recent calls list?' said Finn, folding his arms across his chest.

The hum of the air-conditioning filled the silence.

'Talk to me!' Finn's palm slammed against the surface of the table, and Cynthia jumped in her chair.

She dabbed a sodden paper tissue to her eyes. 'I want a lawyer.'

'I don't care what you want. What the hell have you done?'

She sniffed loudly, and then blew her nose, before looking at him. 'You don't understand.'

Finn frowned. 'What wouldn't I understand?'

His words brought on a fresh bout of sobbing.

Finn gritted his teeth, knowing that if he pushed too hard, Cynthia would clam up, insist on a lawyer being present, and then he'd have nothing to work with.

He turned away from her, walked over to where a tray of glasses and a jug of water stood on a side table, and poured Cynthia a drink.

He looked over to where she sat, her elbow on the table, head in hand, while she used a tissue in her other hand to dab at her eyes.

Her face had paled at his accusation, and now mascara ran down her cheeks.

He knew he was right, that she and Mustafa had been in contact with each other, but he had to tread carefully if he was going to find out the full story.

Finn poured himself some water, emptying the glass in three mouthfuls, and then stood with the cool glass pressed to his forehead.

He couldn't understand why Cynthia might be complicit in Kate's abduction. At the training centre six months ago, the older woman had taken Kate under her wing, especially when he'd been so obnoxious, so what had gone wrong?

He walked slowly back round to Cynthia, giving her time to regain her composure, and set the glass on the table next to her before pulling out a chair.

He spun it around until he could stretch his legs out and crossed his arms. 'Want to tell me what's been going on?'

She sniffed. 'Oh my god, what have I done?'

He shrugged. 'How about you tell me?'

She covered her mouth, as if debating whether to let the words pass. Her fingers fluttered back to the table, and she picked up the water glass, her hands shaking. Taking a sip, she set the glass back down with a clatter.

'It's my fault Kate's been taken,' she said and turned to look at him.

He felt the colour drain from his face, even though he knew she spoke the truth. He fought to keep his voice level. 'Explain.'

'They wanted to know who was closest to Ian. How they could hurt him the most.' She spat out a bitter sob. 'Well it certainly wasn't me he cared about.'

She paused and took another sip of water.

Finn remained silent, knowing that if he interrupted, Cynthia might stop talking and he wouldn't find out what she was confessing to. Although he suspected what was coming, in his heart he hoped he was wrong.

The woman next to him sniffed.

He leaned over the table to where a box of tissues was placed, pulled out a handful and passed them to Cynthia, who nodded, taking them from him.

'All this time,' she said. 'I mean, I know he's had affairs from time to time, but after the last one, I confronted him and he promised to stop,' she waved her hand. 'And then I find out he's back at it.'

She blew her nose again, and Finn sighed inwardly before looking at his watch.

'Out with it Cynthia. What did you do?'

She straightened in her seat.

'I came to an arrangement with Mr Kaan,' she said, and Finn noticed the note of pride in her voice.

'You did *what*?'

A faint smile crossed her face. 'Well, I thought that if Ian couldn't see a good business opportunity when it crossed his desk, perhaps I could help it along a bit.'

Finn's mind started working overtime. 'You weren't in London when Ian called you to tell you Kate had been kidnapped, were you?' he said, rocking back on his chair.

Cynthia shook her head. She took a deep breath before answering. 'I was in Paris.' She looked up and Finn saw a tear tracking down her cheek. 'I – I'd told the gallery I was taking a look at a watercolour we were thinking of purchasing at auction.'

'Is that when they contacted you?'

She shook her head. 'No – no. Kaan came to the gallery in London four weeks ago.'

'What?' Finn let his chair fall forward. 'What did you say?'

She dabbed at her eyes, then glared at Finn, and jutted out her chin. 'I want a lawyer.'

'I told you. I don't care what you want,' said Finn. 'What the hell did you do?'

Cynthia shrugged. 'I think they knew then that Ian would back out of the deal. I don't know why they thought that. They said,' she sniffed, and blew her nose before continuing. 'They said if I helped them persuade Ian to go through with the deal, they'd make me a rich woman in my own right.'

Finn frowned. 'What on earth would you need more money for?'

Cynthia smiled. 'That's exactly what I said to them.' The smile faded. 'Then I found out about his latest affair.'

'How?'

Cynthia shrugged. 'All the old signs were back. Not returning my calls, forgetting that we have a joint credit card so I could see the store purchases.' She broke off and sighed. 'My husband may be a genius when it comes to designing electronics, Finn. He's not exactly blessed with common sense.'

'So *you* came up with the idea of kidnapping Kate?' Finn's voice rose and a surge of anger flashed through his body. He pushed his chair back, standing over her.

Cynthia jumped in her seat and stared up at him, her mouth open, her eyes wide in fright, tears bright on her cheeks.

'Why on earth did you drag Kate into this? What did she ever do to you?' His voice broke. '*Why?*'

Cynthia's bottom lip trembled. 'Because I thought *she* was the one having an affair with Ian,' she said. 'Last time this happened, it was with his bloody secretary. So, what did I have to lose?'

Kate held the chain tightly to her chest and pressed her ear against the rough timber of the door.

She'd been eating the food which the old man had brought to her, when she'd heard raised voices from the level below.

Scrambling up from the mattress, she'd crept to the door, intrigued.

She frowned. Yusuf's voice carried up the stairs, urgent – almost desperate. He paused, and she heard Kaan reply, his tone low and undecipherable.

Kate turned, and rested her back against the door, frustrated that she couldn't hear what the men were saying.

Her gaze roamed the room. Whatever had been said, it didn't change her current situation.

She hurried over to the food, picked up the bowl of bread and stew, and wolfed it down, wiping her hands on her trousers when she'd finished.

She looked ruefully at the stained material, and a fleeting memory of her elation at finding the suit in a New York boutique's sales stock crossed her mind. She shook her head to clear the thought, wondering whether she'd get the chance to shop for a replacement one day.

Her throat tightened, and she coughed, blinking to stop the tears pricking at her eyes from falling.

'Not now,' she murmured.

She put the bowl back down and then crouched next to the iron hoop. She'd managed to dig away at half the mortar now, but the layer underneath was harder, older and tougher to work on.

She wrapped her fingers around the hoop and pulled, then cursed. It still only moved as much as it had when she'd first started.

She stood and stretched, then wandered across to the window and ran her finger across the surface of the sill to complete the day mark she'd been making.

She lifted her finger and counted the marks, even though she knew their number by heart.

She wondered how many she had left. Days? Hours?

She shuddered. When they came for her, what would it be like?

She looked over her shoulder at the locked door and then went back to the mattress and pulled out the concealed nail.

As she inserted it into the crevice she'd created next to the iron hoop, she set her jaw, determined that she wouldn't be chained to the wall when Yusuf returned for her.

'We have to move *now*,' said Yusuf, leaning across the table. 'We haven't had an update for over four hours.'

Kaan eased back in his chair and worked his cigarette lighter between his fingers. He blew smoke towards the ceiling before lowering his gaze.

'It does not matter if your contact has not called. We have what we need. The parts are here in Istanbul, and the exchange will be made within twenty-four hours.'

'Will you let the American woman go free?'

Kaan shrugged. 'I have not yet decided whether she should be allowed to live.'

'She has seen your face.'

'At the moment, she still serves my purpose.' An evil smile crossed his face. 'I presume, then, that you would like the task of dispensing with her?'

Yusuf licked his lips and fondled the knife at his belt. 'I would, that is true.'

Kaan stood and placed his hand on the other man's shoulder. 'Be patient, my friend. I shall have my glory, and you shall claim your prize.'

Chapter 21

'Okay,' said Finn. He put the cardboard box on the desk and gestured to Hart. 'Come here. Walk us through what we need to know.'

Hart pulled open the lid of the box and scooped out some of the small foam packaging cubes. He pulled out a rectangular metal container with the organisation's logo stamped on top of it and set it on the desk.

Unclipping the fasteners, he opened the lid and turned the case round to show Finn and Steve.

They peered inside.

Two slim metal canisters, cigar-like in shape and size, sat in a black velvet cushion.

Finn whistled. 'Very impressive. Is this what you show all your customers?'

Steve punched him on the arm. 'Stop it.' He looked up at Hart. 'Finn's got a point, though. Why's Kaan going to all this trouble to get his hands on these?'

Hart leaned over and carefully lifted one of the canisters out of the case. He held it between his finger and thumb and turned to the other two men.

Finn could see the gleam in the engineer's eyes and realised the man had no concept of the death and destruction he was responsible for with his inventions. Hart's gaze showed nothing but wonder at what his designs could do.

'Inside here is a small concoction of chemicals,' Hart said. 'Separately, they're rendered harmless, but armed with a bomb or a rocket-propelled grenade, they can expel an energy equivalent to several tonnes.'

Steve gave a low whistle and held out his hand. 'Are they safe like this?'

Hart nodded. 'You need a propellant to start the chain reaction.' He passed the other cylinder to Finn. 'At the moment, the chemicals are suspended in their own miniaturised compartments within the casing,' he explained. 'When the propellant causes an initial explosion, breaking open the cylinder, the chemicals mix in the air and give it that extra *boost*.'

Finn ignored the grin on the man's face. It was creepy, to say the least. Instead of bragging about his new invention, designed to take as many lives as possible, he should have been worrying about Kate. All the man seemed to worry about was salvaging his business from the debacle.

He shrugged and forced himself to focus. He handed the cylinders back to Hart, who placed them back into the case and closed the lid. 'We've got twenty-four hours in hand, so let's work through what we're going to do.'

Ian shook his head. 'You don't understand – there isn't time.' He rubbed a hand over his face. 'Kaan changed the deadline. He's demanding the parts by midnight tonight.'

'What the hell? When did that happen?' shouted Finn.

Ian reached into his pocket and held up a mobile phone. 'He called me. I-I have a private number.'

Steve's eyes narrowed. 'Would that be the one Francine used to contact you?'

Hart nodded.

'You asshole. Why didn't you hand it over with the other one when we were fitting the tracking equipment?'

Ian put the mobile phone on the desk and stepped away from it, his face etched with worry while Steve glared at him stonily.

Finn launched himself at Hart.

One minute, he was standing with his arms crossed over his chest, fury in his eyes, the next he'd cleared the space between them. He slapped Hart across his face hard, and then punched him in the gut.

The engineer dropped to the floor, clutching his stomach.

Finn tried to level a kick to the man's kidneys, adrenaline shooting through his veins, fuelling his anger and frustration, before a hand gripped his shoulder, pulling him away.

'That's enough.' Steve's voice cut through his rage. 'Calm down, or you'll end up killing him.'

Finn gritted his teeth and cursed. He spun round and faced Steve, who had his hands up in a defensive position.

'What? You're going to start on me next?'

Finn forced himself to breathe and dropped his hands to his side. 'No.'

'Good.' Steve walked across to Hart and hauled him to his feet.

'That bastard!' said Hart. 'Did you see what he did to me?' He held his nose between his fingers, blood seeping from one nostril.

'Yeah, I did,' said Steve. 'He saved me the trouble. Sit over there and tell us exactly what Kaan said to you, or I'll finish what Finn started.'

At precisely eight o'clock, Emrah Ahmed strode into the room, followed by a team of four men covered head to toe in black clothing.

Hart's jaw dropped at the sight of them. 'What are they doing here?'

'Helping us,' said Steve and shook the intelligence officer's outstretched hand. 'Good to see you. Are the rest of your men in place?'

Emrah nodded. 'You're clear to go whenever you want. Interpol brought me up to speed. With everything.'

He approached Ian, who eyed him suspiciously. 'I am sorry to say this, Mr Hart, but I have placed your wife under arrest for wilfully endangering Kate Foster's life and aiding a terrorist organisation.'

Hart stood, his face pale. 'What do you mean?' He turned to Steve and Finn. 'What's going on? What has she told you?'

Steve folded his arms across his chest. 'When Finn interviewed the garage owner with Emrah earlier today, they found Cynthia's number in the man's mobile phone contact list.'

Hart lowered himself into his chair, his mouth open. He blinked and then stared at Steve. 'What did she say?'

'Finn spoke to her when he returned from interviewing Mustafa. Cynthia confessed, Ian. I'm sorry.' He shrugged. 'She seemed to think it was Kate you were having an affair with.'

He frowned and turned to Emrah. 'Can you keep it quiet in the department until this is over?'

The intelligence officer nodded. 'They will take her to one of the smaller police stations in the city for questioning, away from prying eyes. She will be in no danger.'

'I brought these,' he added, ignoring Hart who was now leaning on his desk with his head in his hands. He turned to Steve and handed over a rolled up tube of paper. 'It'll give you an idea of what to expect.'

Steve took the tube from Emrah and unravelled it across Hart's desk.

'Blueprints,' murmured Finn. 'Now that *is* useful.'

The men pored over the detailed plans of the garage.

'How did you get these?' asked Finn. 'We've been trying to get hold of someone at the planning department for the past couple of hours.'

Emrah shrugged. 'My brother-in-law's cousin works on the city planning committee,' he said. 'I owe him dinner at my house next week.'

He took a sports bag from one of his men outside the door and handed it to Steve. 'We have put together some equipment for you – it is the same as what my men are using.'

Finn walked over, and began pulling out the contents of the bag, testing each piece of kit and familiarising himself with the communications set-up the team would be using.

With half an hour to go until he and Steve planned to leave the office and make their way to the garage where they suspected Kate was being held, he slipped from the room and made his way out to a balcony which overlooked the street.

He leaned on the wrought-ironwork and watched the people and cars moving below, his mind wandering.

He let his head fall between his arms. It had been three years since he'd had to conduct a rescue.

And, like the last mission, he'd be rescuing someone he cared desperately about.

He closed his eyes and inhaled deeply, trying to steady his heartbeat and the sickness in his core. In his mind, he wanted to see Kate as he remembered her the last night of the hostage training.

She'd worn a dress, green silk – totally inappropriate for the setting, but she'd worn it anyway. It had added a touch of glamour to the last night, when everyone could relax without having to worry about being spirited away by the training team.

She'd appeared nervous when she'd walked into the room. When everyone had turned to stare, she'd looked as if she was having second thoughts about her choice of clothing.

Finn had seen the way she'd given herself a mental shake as he'd walked across the floor with a glass of wine.

She'd blushed when he'd leaned down to kiss her cheek.

'You look beautiful,' he'd murmured.

Her hand shook when she took the wine, but she'd smiled and clinked glasses with him.

He'd cursed when Hart had interrupted them, calling everyone to dinner, denying him the chance to apologise for his behaviour during the training. He had then found out that he wouldn't be sitting next to her.

He remembered how the colour of the dress had enhanced the gold flecks in her brown eyes, and how her tanned shoulders caught the light of the candles which Cynthia had insisted on lighting in the middle of the table.

And that kiss on the terrace.

He recalled her pulling away from him, their breathing heavy as she'd gazed up at him, and for a split second, he'd been ready to tell her everything. All his secrets, his terrible history, and why she should go back home.

A noise from the room to their right had interrupted them, and she'd moved away from him, a guilty look across her face.

Cynthia had appeared, asking if everything was okay, and Kate had nodded, turning away from Finn and following the older woman back inside the hotel.

Cynthia. All this because of one woman's misplaced jealousy.

And Hart, a man who designed prototype weapons to improve ways to kill people.

Finn shook his head and vowed that if he found Kate alive and well, he'd spirit her away and never let her out of his sight again. He wouldn't fail – not this time.

He raised his head and turned at the sound of the balcony door sliding open.

Steve stood, silhouetted in the doorframe. 'I thought you might be out here.'

Finn grunted a response, and then turned back to the street. He heard the door close, and Steve joined him at the rail, before peering over the edge.

'Not thinking of jumping, were you?'

'Job's not done yet.'

'Just checking.'

'How are we doing for time?'

'We leave in fifteen.'

'Emrah?'

'He'll set up a cordon once we're in – given that it's an industrial area, it won't take them long. The place should be deserted this time of night.'

'And he won't send his men in early?'

Steve shook his head. 'It's all ours.'

Finn nodded. 'Good.'

Steve turned and leaned against the balcony and folded his arms across his chest. 'Listen, I've been thinking.'

Finn cocked his head and raised an eyebrow.

'Once we're done here and back in Northumbria, I think you should consider taking over the management of the business from me.'

Finn frowned. 'What?'

The other man shrugged, then looked over his shoulder and watched the passing traffic below. 'Well, I'm not getting any younger. Maybe it's time I handed over the reins.'

Finn straightened slowly and held onto the railing, his knuckles white. 'Why would you think that?'

'No particular reason. Just thought it might be time to take a back seat, let you run with it. Got a problem with that?'

'Yes.'

'Why?'

'Because it's *your* business. You built it up from scratch after leaving the SAS. It's doing well. You've got good clients,' he glanced back through the doors, 'most of the time. Why would you want to walk away?'

'Who said anything about walking away? I'll still work every day.'

Finn shook his head and held up his hands. 'I can't deal with this right now.'

Steve shrugged. 'Okay. But do me a favour? Have a think about it when this is over, and let's have a chat when we get home, alright?'

Finn nodded.

'Good. Now let's go rescue your girlfriend.'

Chapter 22

Finn led the way, both men running fast between the buildings which lined the street. Reaching the last structure, they stopped, each taking a deep lungful of air, readying themselves for whatever the next few minutes threw at them.

Steve tilted his head upwards, noticed an open window and put his finger to his lips, nudging Finn, who nodded. The men slunk back into the shadows and used hand gestures to finalise their plan.

Once they were ready, they wasted no more time. Crouching low to the ground to minimise his silhouette, Finn dashed across the entrance to the street that led to the run-down garage business where Kate was held prisoner.

He reached the side of the building opposite, turned and nodded to Steve. The other man began to edge carefully down the street, hugging the buildings and moving slowly. Once he was in place, Finn turned to the garage that was the subject of their planned assault.

He had been surprised that Emrah hadn't joined them in the take-down, preferring instead to observe the action from the comms vehicle parked two streets away.

Emrah had shrugged when asked. 'I am an intelligence officer, Mr Scott.' He waved a hand dismissively. 'I do not get involved in the actual operation. I pay good men to do that.'

As they had left the comms area, hurrying towards their target, Emrah's second-in-command, a man in his thirties by the name of Ali, had murmured under his breath. 'What he didn't tell you is that he's a lousy shot. Almost failed his annual test two months ago.'

Finn had laughed, grateful to the man for trying to ease the tension they had all felt as they prepared for the assault.

His mind coursed through the last moments of the previous operation and sweat broke out across his brow, streaking down his cheek. He shook his head and looked across to where Steve stood.

The other man tilted his head, and then held a palm upwards.

Okay?

Finn nodded, then slid his hand into his black canvas backpack, extracted a wire and detonation charge, and slowly let the backpack drop to the ground behind his legs.

He tightened his grip on the explosives and had begun to move, when two small stones scuffed across the street and hit his boot. He looked back to where Steve was standing and saw the man slowly shaking his head before pointing upwards to the roof above Finn.

He froze.

The men had suspected that the kidnappers would post lookouts to keep an eye on the street, and it was Steve's role to keep watch for them until they were ready to move in.

Finn kept his head low. If the man on the roof above looked down to the street, Finn didn't want him to spot him straight away. Instead, he relied on

Steve to tell him when the way was clear. He held his breath, resisting the urge to look up.

He wondered where the Turkish intelligence officer had positioned his men. They were good – he hadn't spotted anyone on the approach to the building, and even now, they blended with the shadows on the street.

Steve gave him a thumbs-up, and he began to fasten the explosives to the front door. Winding back the wire, he moved backwards until he was clear of the blast zone.

He glanced over his shoulder as Steve jogged across the street to join him.

'On three?'

Finn nodded, counted, and then pressed the button.

The door exploded outwards in a shower of splinters and metal. The men turned away, letting the wooden shrapnel fall around them.

When it had stopped, Finn gritted his teeth, raised his gun and tore through the gaping hole in the wall.

Smoke filled the entranceway, and he fell into a crouch position, Steve covering him from behind, using the outer wall as protection. The sound of running feet echoed along the street as Emrah's men sprinted to join them.

A figure lurched from the shadows of the building, a smoky silhouette lumbering towards them, rifle raised.

Finn fired twice, the suppressor reducing the noise to a low cough, and the man dropped to the floor. Finn didn't check to see if he was still alive – they had to move through the building swiftly. Bending down, he collected the man's rifle, swung it over his shoulder and kept going.

He tapped the communicator attached to his collar which Emrah had insisted they wear, and then cursed as a stream of static filled his ears.

'Comms are down,' he hissed.

Steve tested his set-up. 'Same – must be some sort of jamming system in the building.' He checked over his shoulder at the Turkish military man behind him, who nodded once. 'Okay, we keep going.'

Finn raised his gun in a two-handed grip and sighted it along the passageway. His mind replayed the building blueprints they'd pored over in the office mere hours before. To his right, a staircase led towards the upper two levels. In front of him, a swing set of double doors stood closed, the workshop and mechanics' office beyond.

He held his hand up, using well-rehearsed signals to Emrah's men, who hurried towards the double doors and formed an attack formation.

Finn checked over his shoulder, caught Steve's gaze, and then began to ease himself up the staircase, tread by tread.

He cursed under his breath. In the FBI's Hostage Rescue Team, he'd had state of the art equipment which fed a constant stream of information into his ears from the operation control room. He'd been aided by satellite imagery, infra-red and heat sensor detectors, and a breathing apparatus.

Here, he had a gun he'd never fired, a black cotton mask to cover his face, and a comms system which was currently taking early retirement. He breathed out, willed his heart rate to slow, and concentrated on making his way up the first flight of stairs.

Reaching the landing, Finn dropped to a crouch while Steve covered their rear, each man waiting for the team below to begin their assault, in the hope that it would mask their own movements for a few precious seconds.

The sound of the doors being kicked open downstairs preceded a shouted order and Emrah's men began firing into the garage space below.

Finn and Steve took their cue and began hurrying along the first floor corridor, their guns sweeping left and right into open doorways as they checked one room after another.

Finn's gun automatically jerked upwards at the sound of a shout from further along the corridor, a man emerging from the last room, a rifle pointed straight at them.

Without hesitation, Finn dropped to his knees, firing again. A short sharp blast of sound above his head confirmed Steve had swung round and fired as well.

The man dropped dead to the floor, his weapon sliding across the bare concrete surface.

Finn waited until Steve tapped him on the shoulder, then stood and hurried to where the man lay prone, his eyes closed, blood seeping from two exit wounds.

After checking the last room, the two men hurried to the staircase and began climbing once more.

Finn cursed the comms equipment. Right now, he should have been relaying information back to the rest of the team. Instead, they were running blind, each man responsible for his own safety if the operation turned sour. If things got out of hand, Emrah's men were only seconds away, armed and ready, but with the communication system down, any request for help would have to be in person.

He jerked his head upwards at the sound of the door to the roof slamming shut, and then slowed as they crept up the last flight of stairs, and fell into a crouching position. He turned and signalled to Steve.

A guard stood outside one of the doors, his gun aimed at the stairs, eyes wide and staring. Finn could smell the fear coming off the man and suspected this was the first time the man had been in a combat situation.

He lowered his aim and fired.

The man screamed, then fell to the floor clutching his leg.

'Cover me,' Finn called over his shoulder, pulling a plastic tie from one of the pockets on his jacket. He leaned over the wounded man, grabbed his wrist and quickly secured his wrists to his ankles, and pushed him over.

'That should hold him.'

They both looked up at the sound of running feet coming up the stairs, and stood, guns poised and ready.

The footsteps slowed and Finn spotted hands raised in the air. 'It's me, Ali.'

'Clear.'

The man jogged up the remaining steps, followed by two of his men.

'Situation?'

'One dead downstairs, and this one,' murmured Finn. 'Downstairs?'

'Three dead. No sign of the American woman – or the bomb.'

'What about Kaan?'

'Negative.'

'Are your comms working?'

'No.'

'Shit.'

Finn turned back to the closed door, then at Steve.

'I suppose we'll have to go in then?'

The other man nodded. 'Do it.'

They positioned themselves either side of the door.

'On three?'

'Three.'

Finn fired at the lock, then kicked the door open, the wood splintering in its frame. He dropped to a crouch, his eyes adjusting to the gloom, heart racing, anticipating the shot that would kill him.

Nothing.

He blinked as Steve flicked on the light switch, and then swore.

Chapter 23

Finn tore the mask off his face and threw it to the floor, swearing.

'Dammit, she's not here!'

'We need to find out if there are any clues,' said Steve, placing his hand on Finn's shoulder. 'And quickly.'

Finn closed his eyes, and then shook his head to clear the thoughts which threatened to unhinge him. 'Okay.'

He flicked the safety catch on his gun, tucked it into the webbing on his jacket and began to pace the room with Steve, their footsteps tracing a grid pattern as their eyes scanned the floor.

He ignored the sounds of Emrah's men filing down the staircase, their voices rising through the building as they laughed and joked with each other, the relief of surviving the assault evident.

Tearing the useless comms equipment from around his neck, he pocketed it and began to search the room. Lowering his gaze, he frowned as his eyes swept left and right.

Once he was sure the floor was clear, he strode over to the low bed which had been pushed against one wall. Practised fingers began searching the folds of the thin blankets, looking for something, *anything* which might tell him Kate was okay, that she was still alive.

He threw the blanket to one side, and ran his hands over the surface of the mattress, before lifting the stained pillow and tossing it over his shoulder to Steve.

As Steve took a knife to the pillow and began emptying its contents onto the floor, Finn ran a blade down the length of the mattress and pushed his fingers inside, probing the material.

Frustrated, he stood and kicked the mattress out of the way.

'She was never here, Steve.' He heard the other man sigh and turned to face him. 'She was never here.'

His breath caught in his throat.

On the floor, underneath where the mattress had lain, a gold-plated watch had been secreted.

He bent down, picked up the watch and cradled it in his palm.

'Steve,' he called, his voice shaking. 'Look.'

The man next to him exhaled. 'Is it hers?'

'I think so. Yes. She wore this to the training session. I made her put it into her locker before we did the assault course.'

Steve appraised the room. 'I don't think she was kept here, though. This place has been used as a barracks for Kaan's men.'

They both jumped at the sound of a gunshot from the corridor and rushed back, weapons ready.

Ali stood over the body of the bound terrorist, saw them staring at him, and then shrugged.

'He tried to reach his gun.'

Finn's eye's flickered to where the dead man lay on the floor, his hands still tied, gun out of reach, and then back to the armed policeman.

'If you say so.'

The man nodded, and Finn went back into the room, closely followed by Steve, who raised an eyebrow.

'So much for questioning witnesses then.'

'Wonder if Emrah gave the order?'

'With no comms equipment working? No – that was bloodlust. I've seen it before.'

Finn shook his head. 'It doesn't help us.'

'We should head back to Hart's office before Kaan tries to call him again.'

'Right.' Finn took one last look around the room, and closed his eyes, imagining how Kate's watch would have ended up in the man's possession. He opened his eyes to find Steve staring at him. 'I'm okay.'

The other man nodded, then turned and walked out the door.

'Let's go face the music.'

Finn glanced up as the receptionist appeared in the doorway, and then turned back to Emrah as she discretely closed the door to the room.

For the past twenty minutes, he and Steve had endured the full wrath of the Turkish military officer's anger, while Hart tried to remain invisible, cowering in his chair.

'This is a disaster,' said Emrah. 'My career could be on the line for this.'

'If the comms equipment worked, we could have done a better job,' snarled Finn. 'And some proper back-up support would have helped – we were running around blind in there. Why weren't any of your team watching the building anyway? We identified it as a target hours ago.'

'You let a shopkeeper use you for his own personal vendetta,' said Emrah. 'Just because the garage owner was rude to his son, he chose to implicate him in the kidnapping of the American woman.'

Finn clenched his teeth, his fists balling. 'It was a valid lead.'

'She was never there!' yelled Emrah.

'We had the footage of Mustafa's son dropping off the video,' said Finn. 'He's involved *somehow*!'

'Finn's got a fair point,' said Steve. 'After all, you've got five dead men who are known criminals, and you've still got Mustafa in custody. He must know something about Kaan's plans. Perhaps we could question him again?'

'Pft.' Emrah turned his back on them and walked towards the door. 'I must go back to my office and explain to my superiors why we have failed to apprehend a known terrorist and rescue Ms Foster,' he said. 'You will continue to update me on developments – if and when you succeed in that endeavour.' He paused. 'I will see if I can arrange the interview.'

Finn waited until the door slammed shut, and then exhaled slowly, stretching his neck.

Steve stared at him. 'No outburst? No punching walls?'

'He's right. We screwed up. I screwed up.'
'Maybe.'
'Maybe? We just stormed a building with six Turkish special forces operatives, five blokes are dead, we have no bomb – and Kate is still missing. Which part of that wasn't a screw up?'

'They were there at some point, Finn. We know that much. Someone must know something.'

'So what are you saying – we keep looking?'

'That's exactly what I'm saying.'

'Emrah will kill us himself if he finds out.'

'So let's not tell him. Come on – I've got an idea.'

Finn rubbed his eyes, stretched his arms above his head, then peered at the computer screen once more, his gaze flickering over the text and numbers as he scrolled through the pages.

Across the desk, Steve used his laptop to pull up more documents, printing them out for further analysis.

For the past hour, the two men had worked their way through the tax records, calling in favours and gradually understanding how Mustafa's business worked.

Finn sat with his chin in his hand, tapping his foot on the carpet as he reviewed the paperwork which the police had seized at the property they'd raided.

'You realise he was probably dealing in cash most of the time?'

'Uh huh. Got any better ideas?'

'I'm working on it.'

'Good. In the meantime, keep looking.'

Steve reached over to the printer, pulled a pile of paper across the desk and began flicking through the pages.

'Here we go. Profit and loss statements.'

'By the look of that building, he was making a loss.'

'That's what I would have thought, but these don't look too bad. I mean, he's only just turning a profit, but he's not struggling.'

'What are you – an accountant now?'

Steve glared at him. 'Who do you think does all the tax paperwork for my hostage business? The same business which employs you?'

'Ah.'

'Exactly.'

Finn ran his hand through his hair and tried to concentrate on the lines of numbers on the computer screen.

His mind kept wandering, thinking back to Kate's hostage survival training, worrying about whether she'd remember everything he'd tried to teach her. Whether he'd taught her enough.

At the time, she'd seemed overwhelmed, weak. Now in retrospect, he realised that it wasn't him or the training she'd been battling against – only the memories from her past.

He swallowed, pushing down the panic which threatened to engulf him. The last thing Steve needed now was an irrational, emotional wreck to help him solve this crisis.

'Finn?'

He looked up. 'Sorry – what?'

'You were miles away. Look at this.'

Steve pushed across a well-thumbed set of accounts. 'Look at the sixth line down.'

Finn traced his finger over the page, until he found the cause of the other man's excitement.

Assets.

Finn raised his eyes to Steve, his heart racing. 'He's got more than one business.'

'We were looking in the wrong place.'

Chapter 24

Kate rested her hands on her knees, her back to the wall, listening to the commotion in the room below.

An hour ago, she'd heard a door slam downstairs, and Kaan's voice carried through the building, the anger in his voice chilling her blood.

She'd caught words, phrases – something had gone wrong, but she'd been left alone so far.

She breathed out, then stood, gathering the chain until it was taut in order to silence it, then walked across to the window sill and her dusty markings.

The sun warmed the paint-strewn panes of glass, and she realised her captors were late in bringing her meal. She frowned and checked over her shoulder at the water level in the two litre bottle next to her mattress.

Enough to last until the morning.

Her thoughts returned to Finn. Time and again since her capture, she'd wondered whether she should have said something to him when she finished the training course in England. All too soon, the three days had been over and a minibus had turned up to take them back to the train station.

After shaking Steve's hand, she'd approached Finn, but his goodbyes had been formal, brisk. He'd shaken her hand, then turned his attention back to her new employer, Ian Hart, and she'd felt like she'd been dismissed.

She shook her head. She didn't even have the confidence to give him her phone number back then, so it was highly unlikely that he'd be interested in such a mousy person.

She frowned, thinking what sort of girlfriend Finn Scott would have, and then shook herself mentally. Thoughts like that at the moment would not help.

A shout from downstairs sent her tiptoeing hurriedly across to her mattress.

She sat down and ran her finger over the soft mortar. It was slow work, but she was making progress.

That morning, she'd torn a small hole in the side of her mattress and had begun to insert pinches of mortar dust, shaking the mattress to make sure it didn't spill back onto the floor.

She put her finger into the wall, touching the ironwork. She still had work to do, and so, while the arguments ensued beneath her, she drew out the nail from under the mattress and continued to dig.

'We need to move *now*, Kaan – we can't stay here any longer!'

Yusuf paced the floor of the garage, his voice echoing off the steel double doors to the workshop.

'They're onto us – it's only a matter of time before they find us here!'

Kaan held up his hand to pacify the other man. 'The weapon is nothing without the parts from Hart.' He pointed to where the electrician moved around a metal frame, checking his handiwork for the nth time.

'Without the parts, we won't have the effect we need to draw attention to our cause.'

He turned to the electrician. 'If we detonate it now, what are the damage projections?'

Mehmet scratched his ear lobe. 'If you put it in the location we've discussed, then it will depend on passing traffic. The reinforced concrete of the target structure will absorb a lot of the blast. They would have it repaired within weeks using foreign labour.' He spat onto the floor.

'You see?' said Kaan. 'We wait. It is still hours until the original deadline. As it approaches, they will make more mistakes, until they realise it is hopeless and they must hand over the parts.'

Yusuf strode to where Kaan stood, lowering his face to the other man's. 'Please, listen to yourself. They are going to find us before we reach the deadline. We need to move now.' He raised his eyes to the ceiling. 'And we need to cover our tracks – thoroughly.'

Kaan smiled benevolently, placing his hand on Yusuf's arm. 'Your haste to kill the woman is tainting your common sense my friend. If we go now, we shall be like stoned dogs – running with our tails between our legs while the authorities hunt us down.'

'If we don't go now, they will hunt us down anyway! We have only one man to guard us here. What will happen if we are attacked?'

'There is no chance of that. The trail is cold. Mustafa will not talk.'

'Please, Kaan – listen to reason!'

'No – we stay here. They will meet the original deadline. My contact told me the American man cares for the woman too much to simply abandon her. It shall be his undoing.'

Mustafa Rizman paced the confines of the small room.

Already, he knew that the cell was nine feet by six feet. That it took precisely eight steps to walk from one side to the other. That a further twelve steps were required in order to walk the perimeter, skirting around the metal-framed bed with its thin linen.

The walls were strewn with graffiti – insults, pleas, names – all scratched into the plasterwork over the years.

He scowled at the stained porcelain toilet in the corner of the small room. The drugs which had been pumped into his veins when he was captured had taken their toll on his body, and the stench filled the room despite his attempts to flush it away.

A narrow, barred window at the back of the room allowed light to filter through, casting shadows across the bare concrete floor and over the wall of the corridor beyond the floor-to-ceiling steel bars.

He sat on the edge of the bed, resting his hands in his lap. He had spent the past few hours alone, lost in thought.

The only other prisoner in the cell block had been another man who had called out to him in the first hour, trying to make conversation. He had fallen silent eventually. He had been led away some time ago, accompanied by two guards who had flanked him as he'd walked towards the exit, protesting his innocence.

One of the guards had slapped him round the back of the head, telling him to save his arguments for the court-appointed judge. The man had peered into Mustafa's cell as he'd passed, curious to know who his silent neighbour had been.

Mustafa had turned his back to him, refusing to make eye contact, not caring who he was or what he had done. He hadn't moved again, until he'd heard the security door slam shut behind the small group.

Now, he congratulated himself for keeping Kaan safe, not breathing a word to the authorities about the group's plans already falling into place as the Turkish police desperately searched for clues.

He hawked and then spat onto the floor as he thought of the American who had taken his phone. It had been unfortunate, but none of Kaan's numbers were saved in its memory. He had never met the man – had never been deemed important enough, but his chest swelled with pride at being a part of Kaan's outer circle, and for providing a safe haven while the man finalised his plans.

He turned his head at the sound of a key rattling in the lock of the security door at the end of the passageway, and stood and walked towards the bars of the holding cell.

A guard stood in the doorway, talking to someone out of sight.

Mustafa leaned his head against the bars, craning his neck to see what was going on.

Murmured voices reached his ears, and he watched as the guard nodded once, and then stepped into the passageway, closing the door behind him.

The guard approached his cell and stood for a moment, appraising him.

Mustafa jutted his chin out defiantly, refusing to break eye contact.

The man was a couple of inches taller than him, bulkier, better nourished. The collar of his shirt dug into his neck, his hair slightly longer than the regulatory standard the rest of the guards adhered to.

Mustafa waited patiently, his heart beating heavily in his chest. He desperately wanted to know where they had taken Halim, but he wouldn't beg – not to this man, not yet.

The guard smirked and took a step towards the wall.

'Move to the back of your cell, prisoner. Stand with your hands at your sides at all times.'

Mustafa emitted a noise of derision between his lips, then turned his back on the man and walked unhurriedly to the back of the cell. When he reached the wall, he turned, put his hands at his sides and stared at the guard, waiting.

Satisfied, the guard took a step forward, selected a key from a bunch chained to his belt, and turned the lock.

Sliding the barred section across, he stepped into the cell, his bulk filling the remainder of the small space.

He kept his eyes on Mustafa as he slid the bars back into place, then stood with his arms folded.

The garage owner felt the man's gaze on him, and squirmed inwardly as the guard's eyes travelled the length of his body. He'd heard stories about what went on in the prison – the guards' peculiar tastes and their ideas of having fun.

He held his head up, refusing to look away or break the silence.

The guard moved closer, looked around the room at the repugnant surroundings and moved towards the bed, picking up the thin pillow.

Mustafa felt a trickle of sweat bead at his brow and resisted the urge to wipe it away. He wasn't a fit man and had spent the past twenty years relying on his limited wits rather than his fists. He held his breath as the guard moved towards him, his movements fluid and precise.

As the man drew closer, Mustafa stepped backwards, until he felt the cool wall of the cell press against his shoulders. He swallowed.

'What do you want?'

The guard smiled, lifted the pillow, and launched himself towards Mustafa.

The garage owner's hands beat at his attacker's head and shoulders as the pillow smothered his face, his muffled cries silenced as the guard pressed down harder, grunting with the strain.

Within seconds, Mustafa's hands stopped beating the guard and instead began to pull at the pillow, trying to tear it away from his mouth and nose.

The guard shuffled, repositioning his feet and, leaning against Mustafa's body, pushed the older man into the wall. He ignored the feeble attempts the older man made to fight off the attack. A few moments later, he felt the man's body sag, the arms falling away. He counted the seconds, and then slowly peeled the pillow away.

Underneath, Mustafa's face had contorted in terror, his eyes wide open and bloodshot.

The guard reached out, placed his fingers on the man's neck, and then smiled. He stepped away, letting the body crumple to the floor, before he fluffed up the pillow, obliterating the impression of his victim's head, and tossed it onto the bed. He then slid the bars open and relocked the cell.

He checked over his shoulder at the body on the floor, and then walked back to the security door and knocked once. He handed back the keys.

'It is done.'

Chapter 25

Emrah walked through the door to Hart's office, put his hands in his pockets and turned to face them.

'Earlier this morning, Mustafa Rizman was found dead in his cell.'

It took a moment for the news to sink in. Finn was the first to speak.

'What happened?'

The intelligence officer shrugged 'It looks like he had a heart attack.'

'Did he have a heart problem?'

'We do not know. My team is trying to find out if he had a local doctor we can speak to.' He paused and looked at his fingernails before continuing. 'It does not look good – a terrorism suspect dying in custody. We can only hope that the drugs administered to him were not a contributing factor.'

'Will there be an autopsy?' asked Steve.

'Eventually,' said Emrah and held his hand up to stop their protests. 'There is a – how do you say it? – back-log at the moment. It could be several days before we find out more.'

Finn leaned against the desk and folded his arms. 'He was the best lead we had.' He shook his head. 'I can't believe this.'

Ian stood, his hands shaking. 'This prison cell where the garage owner died – is my wife there? Is she alright?'

'She is being held at a smaller police station,' said Emrah, 'and yes, she is safe – even I do not have clearance to visit her.'

Ian sank back into his chair and ran a hand through his hair. 'Thank god. I mean – I know this mess is partly her fault, but, well... oh my god.'

'What about security camera footage?' asked Steve. 'Did that pick anything up?'

Emrah shook his head. 'Unfortunately there was a malfunction. There is no recording. My second-in-command is currently interviewing the officer that was on duty at the time.'

Finn pushed himself back until he was sitting on the desk, then leaned forwards. He closed his eyes, blocking out the other men's voices.

His whole body ached with exhaustion, the tension locking his muscles. Fuelled by strong coffee and excess adrenaline, the helplessness overwhelmed every thought. He opened his eyes and rubbed a hand over his face.

'How watertight is your investigating team, Emrah?'

The intelligence officer glared at Finn, before his expression softened. 'It is something that has crossed my mind,' he said. 'That is why I am here in an unofficial capacity.' He sighed. 'Corruption is easily paid for – I am doing all I can to find out if I have a traitor in my ranks.'

He walked across to Finn and placed a hand on his shoulder. 'I know how hard this must be for you, Mr Scott. I have seen how you look when you talk of her. We have had our differences, but please – be assured I am doing everything I can to find Ms Foster.'

'I know. Thanks.'

Emrah smiled, and turned to Steve. 'Keep monitoring Mr Hart's telephones. I will contact you as soon as I have any news.'

After he had gone, Steve spun on his heel to face Finn. 'Okay, let's investigate those other businesses.'

Finn pushed himself off the desk and passed the asset list to Steve. 'Alright. There are two more car repair workshops and an internet café. According to the records, Mustafa co-owned that with a younger cousin.'

'And the younger cousin must be more business-savvy. From these figures, it looks like that business has been propping up the other three.'

'Well, they're not going to hide Kate at a café, are they?'

'Depends if it's got a basement, or more rooms above it,' said Steve. He pointed at the laptop. 'Get onto the satellite imagery software – let's check out all three properties.'

Finn minimised the screen he had open, and then selected the software. Typing in the address for the internet café, he blinked to counteract the mild feeling of vertigo as the programme zoomed in to show an aerial shot of the neighbourhood. He then manoeuvred the controls until he was at street level, looking directly at the building.

'That's definitely a no-go,' he said. 'Single storey – it's not much bigger than a shed. Newsagent next door – jewellery store on the other side.'

Steve shook his head. 'No – she won't be held there, you're right. Too much passing foot traffic. Okay – check the two garages.'

Finn typed in the first address while Steve hovered at his shoulder.

The image appeared, and once more, he tweaked the controls so they could view the street. As with the original business, the garage appeared to be derelict, its double workshop closed for business, the single floor above it plain, windows painted over and broken in places. On one side, a warehouse with two panel vans appeared to be open, signage above its doors proclaiming it to be a distribution depot for spices.

On the other side, an empty building stood, derelict, a faded sign advertising rugs mottled and peeling on its façade.

'Alright, pull up the image for the other garage – see if we can narrow it down between the two.'

Finn's hands flew over the keyboard and then he waited impatiently as the image downloaded.

This time, the garage business seemed busier, its doors open and various vehicles parked in front of it.

'Okay – which one?' said Finn. 'Hide her in plain sight above the business which is trading, or at the quieter business?'

'Hang on,' said Steve, walking to the door. 'Back in a minute. Don't touch those two images.'

Finn drummed his fingers on the desk, his foot tapping on the floor while he waited. He knew better than to interrupt Steve when he had a hunch, but they were running out of time.

Kaan's original deadline for the handover for the parts was rapidly approaching, and they'd already shown their hand by raiding the first property. They could only hope that Kaan's need for the parts outweighed any desire to harm Kate while he could still use her as a bargaining tool.

He looked up as Steve jogged back into the room and handed him the USB stick.

'Put that into the computer and play the video – I want to watch it again.'

Finn queued up Kate's message from Kaan and pressed the 'play' icon.

'Scroll through to the last thirty seconds.'

Finn dragged the mouse along the bottom of the screen.

'Stop – play it from there.'

The two men watched the end of the message, Kate's foot tapping out her coded message.

Finn ignored the trickle of sweat running between his shoulder blades and gripped the desk.

'Play it again – from the same place.'

Finn watched in silence until the message ended, then turned to face Steve. He frowned when he saw the other man smiling.

'What?'

'It's the first garage on the satellite imagery.'

'How do you know?'

'Kate told us – she just got her vowels mixed up.'

'What do you mean?'

Steve leaned over and pointed at the screen, Kate's image frozen on the replay.

'She didn't mean 'space',' said Steve. 'She meant *spice*.'

Finn's head shot round to look at the satellite imagery on the laptop, to the warehouse next door to the garage. 'She can smell the spices.'

He turned back to Steve. 'Kaan's trying to cover his tracks, isn't he? He got to Mustafa before Emrah could interview him again.'

'Do we call Emrah?'

Steve shook his head. 'No time. And I don't fancy a repeat of this morning's disaster if we're wrong.'

'I'll go get our gear together.'

'Okay – I'll grab a couple of Hart's security guys – see what intel they can give us about that area around the garage. We have to move fast.'

'When do you want to go in?'

Steve glanced at his watch and then back at Finn, an uneasy expression etched across his face.

'Before nightfall. After that, it's too easy to move a body.'

Chapter 26

Finn ignored the commotion around him and began methodically setting out the equipment they would need onto the floor around the office.

Steve had followed suit, although his kit comprised a lot more communications and first aid equipment.

Finn's was all weaponry.

He laid out the knives, gun and stun grenades, and then pushed aside the heavy-duty equipment. He needed to be able to move fast, and too much equipment could mean the difference between a successful mission or a disaster.

Standing up, he stretched and then made his way over to Hart's desk which had been swept clear, its contents strewn across the floor. In their place, a large map of the area around the garage and spice warehouse had been laid out, its corners pinned down, black pen marks covering its surface where the men had planned their assault.

'We're going to have to work quickly once we're in,' said Steve. 'The garage is only a couple of blocks from a quayside. We can't recce the area before we go otherwise we could alert Kaan that we're onto him. We have to assume that he'll have a means of escape – a boat for instance.'

'We could alert the police, ask for a water patrol to be present.'

Finn glanced at the security man who spoke, then back to Steve. 'It's a good idea.'

'We'll phone Emrah right before we go in. He's right – if there's a leak in his department, then we don't want to alert Kaan to our presence. As the saying goes, better to ask forgiveness after the event…'

'True. And they'll have water patrols up and down that part of the Bosphorus anyway, so they should be able to get there within minutes.'

'Have you got the bomb parts?'

Finn patted the webbing across his bulletproof vest. 'Here.'

'Put them in the safe.' Steve checked his watch. 'We've only got a few hours until the deadline expires – we need to move.'

After running through final tests of their equipment, Finn checked that Hart's security detail were ready to monitor the phones in their absence. He picked up his backpack and swung it over his shoulder. Standing in the middle of the room, he took a deep breath, before letting it pass his lips.

'You ready?'

He turned at Steve's voice, and then nodded. 'Let's go.'

Finn manoeuvred the car through the late afternoon commuter traffic, the car's tyres kicking up a cloud of dust which obliterated the view out the back window.

Steve scrolled through his contacts until he found Emrah's number and held his thumb over the 'call' button.

'Are you ready for this?'

'No. Do it anyway.'

A dial tone sounded, followed by the sing-song tones of the number being dialled, and then a ring tone filled the vehicle.

'Turn the volume down,' said Finn. 'This could hurt.'

The phone rang three times before the intelligence officer answered.

'Emrah.'

'It's Steve Orton. I've got Finn on speaker with me.'

'What is it? Have you found anything?'

'We think so, yeah.'

Finn glanced sideways as the man took a breath to psych himself up to deliver the news.

'We went through Rizman's accounts – turns out he had four businesses. Three garages and an internet café he owned with a cousin.'

'You're stalling,' hissed Finn, turning the wheel and overtaking a slow-moving moped.

Steve held his middle finger up, and then turned his gaze back to the mobile phone in its cradle. 'We got the wrong garage this morning. Not sure if you got the message from your office when we sent you a copy of Kate's video yesterday, but she used Morse code to try and tell us where she was.'

'I hadn't. Go on.' Emrah's voice had dropped to a low murmur.

'She got her vowels mixed up in her message. We think – we believe – she's being kept hostage at another of Mustafa's garages – next to a spice warehouse near the Zeytinburnu port terminal.'

Finn swerved the car between two trucks and placed his foot on the accelerator. 'We're two minutes out from the target,' he murmured.

Steve held up his hand. 'Emrah?'

'How sure are you?' asked the intelligence officer.

'We're on our way there now. It'd be good if you could muster one of your teams to meet us there to help with the take down. A water patrol would be a good idea too.'

A long silence filled the air.

Finn stared at the phone. 'You can feel the 'fuck off' vibes from here,' he whispered.

Steve leaned forward to check the call was still connected, then sat back in his seat and waited for the onslaught.

'You are on your way there now?' Emrah exploded. 'Without permission from me? What the hell do you think you're playing at?'

Steve rested his head back against his seat and closed his eyes.

'Stand down immediately!'

'No can do, sorry,' said Steve. 'We're fully committed to this operation now.'

'You will do as I say,' hissed Emrah. 'You could be killed going in there alone!'

Finn leaned over and rubbed his finger over the phone's microphone. 'Sorry, Emrah, you're breaking up... What did you say?'

He looked over at Steve, who winked at him, leaned forward and blew gently across the microphone. 'We must have entered a low signal area, Emrah – do what you can for us, okay?'

He pressed the 'end' key and leaned back in his seat. 'That was easier than I thought.'

'We are *so* going to get our arses kicked if we're wrong about this.'

'Then let's hope we're not wrong. I don't think we're going to get a third shot at this, do you?'

In reply, Finn gritted his teeth, then swung the car a hard left, gunned the engine once to gain some distance from the main road, and then braked hard. He turned the key towards him and checked the rear view mirror.

Nothing.

For a moment, both men sat still and listened to the ticking of the engine as it cooled.

'You ready?'

Finn held up his hands. They shook a little, and his pounding heart ached between his ribs, but he knew he would go on.

For Kate, he'd do anything.

'Yeah. I'm ready.'

'Come on then.'

Shouldering their backpacks, the two men checked their guns, made sure they had spare clips within easy reach, and then locked the car and jogged the short distance to the street where the garage business was based.

Finn slowed as he approached the end of the alleyway, and then peered around the corner of the building. The garage was fifty metres up the road, on his side of the street. The setting sun cast a pink glow over the stonework of the surrounding warehouses as afternoon turned to evening, the sunset eclipsed by the buildings to his rear.

Steve tapped him on the shoulder. 'How's it looking?'

'No-one's around at the moment. The spice business is all closed up for the day. No cars outside.'

'There's nobody in the alleyway behind us either. We'd better move quickly.'

Both men turned as, one by one, muezzins in the distance began the call to prayer.

'Perfect timing,' said Finn and pulled out an earpiece from his pocket, before fitting it to his right ear. He pressed once on a microphone fixed to his collar.

'Alpha Two to base, can you hear me?'

'Loud and clear.'

Hart's head of security was keen to redeem himself after Kate's kidnapping, volunteering to stay behind and monitor the communications feed on Finn's laptop, which included video recording via cameras mounted to the men's armoured vests.

'Any phone calls?'

'Negative. Nothing since you left the office. Haven't had reports of anyone arriving or leaving the building for the past hour, either.'

'Holed up inside somewhere,' said Steve. 'Good.'

'Okay,' said Finn. 'We're going in. Radio silence unless we ask you a question, or you need to tell us something urgent, got that?'

'Got it.'

'Alpha Two out.'

Finn turned to Steve. 'Are we ready?'

'As we'll ever be.'

'Alright, let's do this.'

Finn checked the safety on his gun was in the 'off' position, and then led Steve in a crouched run towards the garage, hugging the walls of the buildings as they completed their approach.

According to the plans which Hart's security men had found, a side door led to the stairwell inside the building and to the garage workshop beyond.

Finn, closely followed by Steve, scurried round the side of the building and stood to one side of the closed door.

He reached out his hand and turned the door knob.

Locked.

Steve crouched down, slid his backpack down his arm, and then reached inside and pulled out a set of lock picks.

Both men had agreed that to enter the building as noisily as the last one, with no support team in place, would have been suicidal. Instead, they planned to use a soft approach until it became absolutely necessary to use force.

Steve selected a pick, then inserted it into the lock and wriggled it from side to side. As the metal scraped against the rusty insides, a trickle of sweat ran down the side of his face.

Finn gritted his teeth, and checked over his shoulder. Outside the building, in daylight, they were exposed. They needed to get inside fast.

He turned at a grunt from Steve, who then smiled as the lock gave way.

Finn cocked an eyebrow at him, and he nodded, standing back and readying his weapon.

Finn turned the door handle, swinging the door outwards, and then both men slipped into the gloom, keeping as low as possible.

Blinking rapidly to adjust his eyesight, Finn turned his head left and right, getting his bearings. He pointed towards a double set of doors, guessing that they led to the garage workshop. As Steve covered their backs, he slowly pushed the door open, keeping low.

A soft blue hue filled the space, the dirty windows filtering the waning sunlight and illuminating the workshop.

The men crouched and entered the garage, watching for movement in the shadows. They walked a quick perimeter of the space, careful not to touch anything for fear of making a noise to alert their enemy, and returned to the double doors.

'Anything?'

Steve shook his head. 'No tangoes, but there's a bloody great homemade bomb sat over in the corner.'

'Is it armed?'

'Negative.'

'Okay, let's keep going.'

'Hang on.'

Steve bent down, picked up a length of metal piping and slipped it through the handles of the closed doors to stop anyone from following them through the garage. He turned and grinned at Finn.

'I hate surprises.'

Chapter 27

Kate bit her lip and sawed at the mortar with the nail.

Minutes ago, the sharp end of the nail had split away, worn through by the pressure she had to exert to work away at the wall.

Cursing, she'd pulled out the broken piece with her little finger, and then went back to work. Frustratingly, she could feel the iron bolt becoming looser, and managed to wriggle it from side to side, yet it still wasn't ready to yield.

She squinted in the fading light as the sunset tipped over the back of the building. She couldn't stop. Her life depended on escaping from her captors – and soon.

The argument downstairs had fallen silent hours ago, a door had slammed shut, and she'd heard a car engine power away.

Yet they still hadn't returned with any food or fresh water.

She wiped the sweat from her eyes, pushed her hair out of the way and pulled the nail free, bending closer to the wall to check her progress.

Grasping the iron bolt between her fingers, she pulled hard, and felt it give a little more. She tried again, and this time a cloud of dust poured from the hole.

She fell back onto her backside in surprise, staring at the bolt she held in her hand, remnants of mortar hugging its surface.

For a moment, she sat still, completely shocked that she'd managed to free herself. A smile crept across her face.

'Yes!' she hissed, and then instinct kicked in.

She still had to get out of the room.

Finn moved stealthily towards the door to the right of the garage workshop, pressing his back to the wall nearest the door handle, and then tested it.

The door stuck in its frame before opening fully, the hinges rusted and creaking.

So much for the element of surprise.

Finn kicked the door the rest of the way open and fell into a crouch, his gun sweeping the room. Satisfied it was empty he entered the space, closely followed by Steve.

Noticing the table in the middle of the room, he spun round, appraising his surroundings.

'This is where they filmed her,' he whispered.

'We've got to keep moving, Finn.'

Leaving the room, the two men worked their way quickly up the flight of stairs, their footsteps on the steel muffled by the soft soles of their shoes.

Reaching the landing, Finn swept his gun in front of him, and then caught a movement out the corner of his eye.

'Down!'

He ducked as a bullet embedded itself into the plaster next to his head a split second before he heard the report of the gun which had fired it.

Steve aimed from a couching position, firing his gun at the place where he'd seen the muzzle flash.

Finn heard a grunt, followed by another gunshot which kicked up dust next to his face.

'That was too close,' he grumbled. 'Back!'

He and Steve shuffled back to the stairs, keeping low. As they moved, a shadow detached itself from the end of the passageway, ran to the door and slid the bolts back.

The man grinned, exposing rotten teeth, then kicked the door open and aimed his gun at the person inside.

Finn yelled, rushed up the stairs, and fired.

Then he heard the sound of glass shattering, and a scream.

He ran, praying he wasn't too late.

Kate had jumped as a crash vibrated through the wall behind her. Her heartbeat racing, she gathered the chain in her hand, and moved swiftly to the door.

Raised voices, urgent and panicking echoed through the building, muffled through the wooden surface.

Kate jerked her head away from the door at the sound of a second loud noise and realised it had been a gunshot.

Frantically, she scanned the room, and then her gaze fell to the window.

She'd have to break the glass to try to escape, and she realised that as soon as she did, she wouldn't be able to change her mind – the noise would bring her guards running if they weren't involved in the commotion she could hear downstairs.

She tested the weight of the iron hoop in her grip, then using the chain, she swung it over her head until it smashed through the panes of glass.

She glanced over her shoulder, but realised she was out of time. There was no turning back now that she'd started.

Her breath caught in her throat. Footsteps. Someone running up the stairs in her direction.

She moved quickly, the footsteps drawing nearer, running towards her cell. She peered up at the window, then stepped back and jumped, her fingers snagging the sill before she tumbled to the floor.

Cursing, she moved back to the middle of the room, and then ran at the wall, leaping forward at the last minute. This time, she gained a hold on the sill, obliterating the day marks she had been making. Winded, she began using her feet to push herself upwards, until her head drew level with the opening and then hauled herself up until she could hook her elbows over the edge.

She caught her breath, ignoring the pain which shot through her ankle, then gripped the iron hoop and broke the remaining glass out of the panes, and pulled the flimsy frame out of the gap. Rotten wood fell away between her fingers, and she dropped it to the floor below.

Craning her neck, she peered outside, a cool breeze ruffling her hair as she leaned out of the opening. She narrowed her eyes and surveyed the ground beneath the window.

The room was on the top level of the building, with a metal fire escape winding its way up to the roof. The ironwork was too far away to reach though, so Kate shook her head and kept searching. Directly below, a pile of refuse bags awaited disposal, the stink reaching her nostrils and making her gag.

It felt strange knowing that she was moments away from freedom, or death. Resolute, she began to turn her body on the sill so her feet pointed out the window first. She recalled her father once telling her that if she ever needed to escape her bedroom in the event of a fire as a child, she should hang out the window as far as she could, and then drop, and roll on impact to avoid breaking any bones.

Except then, there had been a privet hedge below her bedroom window to break that fall.

Now, only a concrete pavement welcomed her if she missed landing on the refuse bags.

What if she broke her leg? How would she escape then? Were there open businesses or houses nearby? Were the people friendly, or would they return her to her captors?

She swallowed, knelt on the sill and mentally prepared herself for the fall.

She spun round at a sudden noise from outside the locked door.

A gunshot, loud in the enclosed space, reverberated through the building. Kate cried out, pulled herself through the window and looked down at the bags, wondering if they'd break her fall.

She glanced over her shoulder in fright at a loud crash from behind. The door was splintering, a deep cut tearing through the wooden surface, before a metallic jangle of bolts tore through the noise. The handle began to turn, stopped and then the door shook as it was kicked from the other side.

Kate turned in the window opening, her feet dangling in the air. As the door fell open, a man stood silhouetted in its frame. She recognised one of Kaan's men, his face livid, moments before a second gunshot reverberated around the room, and he fell forward, a deep exit wound blossoming across his chest moments before a bullet ricocheted off the plaster above Kate's head.

She screamed, her hands slipping across the window sill, and fell.

Chapter 28

Finn yelled as he saw Kate disappear from view. He pushed his way through the door, climbed across the dead man's body and ran to the window, fearing the worst.

He hauled himself through the opening, cursing as his wide shoulders scraped the walls, and looked down.

Kate hung from the chain around her wrist, the iron loop hitched over a metal beam which protruded from the building a storey below. She swung round in a circle, both hands wrapped around the chain. She raised her head at the sound of his voice.

He grinned. 'Hey, Rapunzel, you're not supposed to throw *yourself* out the window.'

Kate glared at him. 'Where the hell have you been?'

She broke off and cried out as the metal beam shuddered and creaked with her weight. Mortar dust fell from around its surface, tumbling to the hard ground below.

Finn stopped smiling as Kate's face contorted with fear. 'Let's get you up.'

'Hurry – I don't think this is going to hold for much longer!'

Finn looked over his shoulder as Steve ran through the door and slid back off the window sill into the room.

'What's going on?'

'She fell through the window. I'm going to pull her back up. Cover me.'

'Okay. Be quick – there might be reinforcements.' He threw his backpack towards Finn before turning his back to the window and pacing the room, his eyes alert for any movement outside the door, his finger on the trigger of his gun.

Finn opened the pack and extracted a length of rope and a grappling hook. Striding over to the window, he tied the hook to the rope and then heaved himself back onto the window sill and leaned out.

'How're you doing?'

'Hurry, Finn,' Kate gasped, her body weight twisting her in the air. She pointed her feet towards the wall to stop her body from spinning and stared up at him. 'What are you going to do?'

He pushed the rope through the opening and let it fall down the wall before the grappling hook caught the inside of the window sill and held. Next, he swung the free end of the rope towards Kate.

'Grab onto this,' he said. 'It'll take some of the strain off the beam.'

He waited until she'd managed to get a firm hold. 'Okay, I'm going to pull you up,' he said. 'Use your feet to walk up the wall to help me.'

Kate waited until the slack had been taken up by Finn, and then began to place the soles of her feet on the stonework of the building. When her feet slipped, Finn held the rope tight until she managed to stop herself from spinning, and then found new purchase. With Finn feeding the rope through his hands at the other end, she made quick progress.

'Wait!' she called. 'I need to unhook my wrist.'

Finn peered through the window and watched as, gritting her teeth, Kate strained her body across the building.

She leaned further, and tugged the iron loop off the metal beam which had saved her from plummeting to the street below. Gathering it up, she slipped it over her wrist and then clutched onto the rope with both hands, a sigh of relief escaping her lips, before she turned her face to Finn.

'Okay – pull me up.'

Within seconds she'd reached the window sill.

Finn reached through and grabbed her arms.

'It's okay, I've got you – I've got you,' he panted, sweat pouring down his face. 'Steady.'

Kate wriggled through the gap in the wall, dropped the chain and iron loop onto the floor and allowed Finn to pull her down to the ground.

Except when she got there, he didn't let go.

He couldn't. Not yet.

He pulled her closer and enveloped her in his arms, burying his face in her hair.

They both jumped at the sound of a cough.

'Folks, I'm really happy for you, but we have a bomb to sort out and a bad guy to find.'

Kate turned and smiled. 'Hi, Steve.' She wiped away the tears which covered her cheeks.

He held his hand up in greeting and spoke to Finn. 'Focus. This is where it could still go pear-shaped.'

'I think they must have living quarters on the level below,' said Kate. 'That part of the building has always been quiet compared with the garage downstairs.'

'Okay,' said Steve. 'I'll go in search of Kaan – you go back and guard the bomb.' He caught the backpack which Finn threw to him and turned to go.

'Steve?'

'What?'

'Be careful,' said Finn. 'We all leave by the front door, right?'

'Right.'

He turned to Kate. 'Ready?'

She grasped his outstretched hand.

He paused. 'You do exactly what I say, understood?' He swallowed. 'No time to ask why – just do it, okay? Your life depends on listening to me. I can get you out of here.'

She nodded.

'Come on then.' He checked the exit first, his gun held steady in front of him, before leading her through the door.

Plaster hung from the walls and ceilings along the passageway, and as they approached the staircase, he noted the pockmarked welds to the steel frame where it had been repaired over time.

As they descended, Finn pushed Kate behind him, keeping her close to the wall. Steve glanced over his shoulder as they reached the next floor, gave Finn a thumbs-up and disappeared into the gloom, hunting his prey.

Finn pulled Kate after him, slowly descending to the ground floor. Reaching the lower level, he turned to her.

'Should we be expecting anyone else?'

She closed her eyes. 'There's a short guy, middle aged – I think he's the bomb-maker. Kaan, and another man – younger.' She shuddered. 'Nastier – about your height and build. They called him "Yusuf". He has a knife.'

'Yusuf. Okay, good – I think everyone else is out of action.'

He pulled Kate across to the room next to the stairs and pulled out a chair for her. 'Stay here. Don't move.' He reached into his backpack and pulled out a pepper spray and handed it to her. 'You know what to do with this if you need to.'

She nodded, and took it from him.

He realised her hands were shaking. He squeezed her shoulder, and then turned and hurried back to the double doors leading through to the garage. He removed the metal pipe from the door handles and slowly pushed them open.

Once he was through, he edged the doors closed again, his eyes adjusting to the dim light.

Hugging the wall, Finn worked his way round the workshop, stepping over car jacks and tools which had been left lying around. Passing shelves laden with spare car parts, he checked over his shoulder and frowned.

The double doors were now open.

A man stood on the threshold, silhouetted by the low light from the passageway, a rifle in his grip.

'I know you're in there!'

The man's voice shook, and Finn noticed how his hands trembled on the weapon.

He smiled and began to edge his way towards the figure, his gun ready.

His head jerked up at a noise from the doorway. A taller man had appeared behind the first and seemed to be talking to him, before his arm snaked around his neck and jerked once, hard.

Finn exhaled through his teeth as blood from the victim's neck spurted upwards and over the concrete floor.

He cursed as the second figure used the man's body as a shield, moving into the darkness of the garage, until Finn lost sight of him.

Tightening his grip on his gun, Finn shuffled past the shelving units, his heartbeat pounding in his ears, his mind racing.

'I know you're in here,' the man's voice called out. 'And I will find you.'

Too late, he turned at the sound of running feet, and then growled as Yusuf emerged from the shadows, raising a length of metal piping, before he lunged forwards.

The blow caught him below his ribs, and he collapsed to the floor with a grunt, clutching his right side. His gun slid away from him across the concrete surface.

He pushed himself up to a crouching position and began crawling away, but Yusuf laughed, and then aimed a kick to his kidneys.

Finn rolled, the tip of Yusuf's boot scraping his skin. Sucking air into his lungs, he pushed himself upright, raised his fists and moved his body into a defensive stance.

As Yusuf raised the metal pipe once more, Finn stepped quickly into the man's attack, punched the arm which held the pipe and swung a kick at the man's shins, before backing away.

Yusuf yelled in surprise, but his grip on the metal pipe only lessened for a moment. He lifted it again. His breath hissed through his teeth as he circled his adversary.

As the pipe swung towards him, Finn ducked and charged. He wrapped his arms around the other man's waist and drove him backwards into the shelves.

Yusuf grunted with the impact.

Finn stepped back, aiming a punch at the man's nose.

Too late, his peripheral vision spotted the pipe bearing down.

Finn cried out with the impact and fell to the floor. He rolled onto his back and glared at his assailant.

Yusuf smiled, patting the metal piping in his hand, and then reached into his belt and pulled out the bloodied knife, twisting it in the moonlight so that its blade glinted in Finn's face.

'I'm going to enjoy this,' he snarled.

He held the knife to Finn's right eye as he ran his other hand over his clothing, reaching into pockets and folds of fabric until satisfied that he carried no weapons.

He grinned at Finn, tracing the blade down the hostage specialist's body until it rested under his rib cage, and then bent to his ear.

'Now you will pay for what you have done,' he whispered.

Chapter 29

Kate heard Finn cry out in pain and stood, knocking the chair to the ground.

She rushed to the door and peered around the corner of the wall. The passageway remained empty. She carefully walked along the length of the wall to the doors which led through to the garage.

Once she was sure she wouldn't be seen, she continued to sidle up the length of the passageway, making her way to the workshop area, then froze.

A man's legs stuck out across the threshold of the room, his rifle on the floor.

Kate ignored the temptation to retch at the sight of his dead eyes and the torn skin around his neck, and edged quietly towards the door. A groan stopped her heart.

Finn.

'Wait,' he said, and she could hear the pain in his voice.

She closed her eyes and took a deep breath, but before she could decide what to do next, a man's voice carried through the room.

Yusuf.

Kate glanced down at the chain hanging around her wrist, and made sure the end of it was gathered up so it wouldn't fall to the floor and give her presence away.

Satisfied, she crept closer to the door. She realised she'd have to take a risk and peer round, to see what state Finn was in.

'You cannot stop me,' said Yusuf. He held a length of metal piping and a knife, pointing both towards Finn, who writhed on the floor, clutching his shoulder.

'The bomb's useless without the parts,' panted Finn. 'Give it up.'

Yusuf smiled. 'It's not useless. It's primed and ready,' he said. 'It won't be as powerful, but it will work.'

Kate looked behind to make sure she hadn't been followed, and then held onto the door frame and leaned forward, twisting her body to face the room.

Yusuf stood with his back to her, only a few metres away. He paced back and forth, then seemed to lose interest in Finn and walked over to where a home-made bomb had been constructed.

Yusuf smiled, leaned down to the weapon and flicked a switch.

Kate's eyes widened at the sight of a digital timer, the red numbers flaring in the gloom.

'No, don't!' said Finn. 'You'll kill innocent people!'

'You are too late,' said Yusuf, pressing another button. 'You will die here.'

He turned, and Kate pulled herself back behind the doorframe, not daring to breath. Her heart thundered in her chest as the countdown began.

'I shall have great pleasure in killing you,' said Yusuf, and Kate's blood chilled at the smoothness of the man's voice. 'It's a shame that you won't live to see what I have in mind for your woman.'

She heard him pacing back and forth once more, and risked a glance into the room. Yusuf stood with his back to her, preening in front of Finn.

Kate began to loosen her grip on the chain in her left hand, slowly lowering it until the metal hoop on the end began to swing in her grip.

Finn's eyes flickered towards her and back to Yusuf in a split second.

Kate built up the momentum in the chain, testing the weight, fighting down the fear which rose in her chest. Adrenaline poured through her body, turning the fear into anger.

Finn began to speak. 'Listen, Yusuf – I'm sure my people can help you. Make the authorities understand,' he said, pretending to panic. 'I mean, I've seen Kate – you've fed her, sheltered her – I'm sure they'll take that into account.'

Yusuf threw back his head and laughed.

Kate nearly dropped the chain in fright at the evil underlying the man's laugh, and was grateful that at that moment, Finn let out a loud groan to distract Yusuf from the noise.

Yusuf began to test the weight of the pipe in his hand. 'I will not beg to the authorities,' he said. 'But you will beg by the time I have finished with you. You will beg for your death.'

Kate launched herself forwards, swung the chain and watched, fascinated as the iron hoop connected with the back of Yusuf's skull with a sickening thud.

The man crumpled to the floor, the metal pipe clattering to his side.

Finn rolled over into a crouching position and eased himself up, hissing through his teeth.

Kate ran to him, and he pulled her into his arms.

'That was quick thinking, well done,' he said. He looked across the room to the armed bomb. 'We've got ten minutes. We need to get out of here.'

He began to lead Kate from the room, pushed her through the open doorway, and then turned back.

'Finn? What are you doing? We need to go – now.'

'Hang on. I've got an idea.'

She watched while he strode over to where Yusuf lay on the floor, out cold, then grabbed the man under his arms and began to pull him across the floor towards the bomb.

'Finn?'

'No time to explain – grab his feet. Hurry.'

Kate lifted the man by his ankles, nearly dropping him when he groaned.

'Quickly,' said Finn. 'He's coming round.'

'What are you going to do?'

'Trying a little persuasion,' he grinned. 'Appeal to his better nature.'

'Really?' Kate frowned. 'You think he's got a better side?'

Finn shrugged. 'No, but it's worth a try. Here. This'll do.'

They set the man's body next to the bomb. Kate couldn't help looking at the timer.

It had dropped to seven minutes.

'Finn, whatever you're planning to do, you need to hurry up.'

'I know.'

Kate watched, her mouth open, as Finn pulled a set of handcuffs from his back pocket and slipped one end through the metal frame which held the bomb together. He then bent down, picked up Yusuf's wrist and stretched the man's arm until he could slip his hand through the other cuff.

Yusuf's eyes flickered open at the sound of the cuffs as they ratcheted closed.

Finn crouched down and patted the man's face. 'Come on, Yusuf, we're running out of time here.'

He struck the man harder across the face, until his eyes lost their dazed expression. Finn pointed to the timer, which had now dropped to six minutes.

'Stop the clock.'

Yusuf's eyes narrowed, and he shook his head. 'Go to hell,' he spat.

'No thanks,' said Finn, standing up. 'But you can.' He turned to Kate. 'Let's go.'

Finn held her hand and began to lead her from the room, away from Yusuf and his bomb.

The entrapped man began to struggle, thrashing his arms as he tried to break loose.

Kate reached the door, and then stopped at the sound of a faint metallic sound upon the concrete floor. 'Wait.'

Finn frowned as she hurried back to Yusuf, the pepper spray pointed at him.

She knelt down, found what she was looking for and held it up to show Finn.

'A necklace?' he said, raising an eyebrow.

'They stole it from me,' she said. 'It fell out of his pocket. I'm taking it back.'

As they hurried away, they could hear Yusuf frantically rattling the handcuffs, trying to loosen his wrist and get away from the weapon.

Kate heard the man whimper as they walked through the door, then felt Finn shove her in the shoulder so she couldn't turn back.

'I can't believe you just did that,' she hissed under her breath.

'Neither can Yusuf,' said Finn. 'Come on. We've got to find Steve and get out of here before that thing blows.'

'Do you think he'll stop the timer?'

Finn shrugged, and began running up the steel staircase to the next level.

Kate shook her head, and then followed.

A gunshot reverberated through the building, and they stared at each other.

'Steve!' Finn grabbed her hand and pulled her up the staircase with him to the next floor.

Her stomach heaved when she saw Steve lying on the floor of the room on the first floor. His blood had stained the surface a deep red, and his face had turned pale and clammy.

'Steve?'

Kate rushed over to join Finn and crouched down.

'Bastard jumped me and shot me in the leg,' Steve gasped.

'Where's Kaan?'

'Escaped. Back staircase.' He groaned.

'Come on,' said Finn. 'Up you get. Guess I'm going to have to carry you out of here, huh?'

He manoeuvred Steve's body into a fireman's lift and turned to Kate.

'Okay – go. Don't turn back. Get down those stairs, out the front door and to the end of the street as fast as you can.'

'What about you?'

'Right behind you – go!'

Chapter 30

Adrenaline and fear kept Kate going through the building, then down a short flight of concrete steps which led to a doorway. She pushed the door open, bent down and picked up a brick which lay amongst a small pile of cigarette ends. Once she was sure the door wouldn't snap shut and slow Finn and Steve's escape, she turned and fled.

She ignored the pain in her ankle as she ran down the middle of the street. She strained her ears but couldn't hear Finn behind her since they'd left the confines of the building.

At the end of the street, she stopped and turned, leaning forward until she could rest her hands on her knees. She panted hard, her lungs desperate for oxygen, her mind light-headed, while her eyes sought out Finn. She saw him a few hundred metres away, lurching from side to side with Steve's weight while he doggedly ran towards Kate and away from the bomb.

As she watched Finn approach, she imagined the timer's final countdown. Were they far enough away? Her gaze wandered to the garage at the end of the street, then fell back to Finn as he reached her.

She helped him lower Steve carefully to the ground, and then they stood and peered around the edge of the building.

'How much?' asked Finn.

'What?'

'How much are you willing to bet Yusuf will stop the timer?'

'Do you think he will?'

Finn folded his arms across his chest and nodded.

Kate frowned. 'This is a stupid game.'

'Five bucks?'

'Deal.'

His touch was electric to her skin, and she noticed how he kept hold of her hand longer than necessary. Then he blinked and checked his watch.

'Five seconds.'

Kate turned and looked at the building which had been her prison for the past five days as she counted the seconds under her breath, her words echoing Finn's.

'...three, two, one, *zero*!'

Silence.

Then Finn started to chuckle.

Kate exhaled, all the strain in her shoulders easing as she turned to Finn and smiled.

'He stopped the clock.'

'Sure did. I guess once his boss ran out on him, he didn't like the idea of being a martyr after all.'

He placed a hand on her arm and gently pushed her aside before crouching down next to Steve.

The older man's eyes fluttered open, and then focussed on Finn.

'Did you stop the bomb?'

Finn nodded. 'I had some help.'

Kate joined them, and noticed the dark pool of blood blossoming across Steve's thigh.

Finn frowned and carefully lifted the torn fabric away from the wound, his jaw set as Steve groaned in pain.

'Sorry – need to take a look at this.'

He touched the fabric and turned to Kate.

Her brow wrinkled as his eyes travelled the length of her body, before returning to meet her gaze. He blinked and shook his head.

'What?'

'We need something to apply pressure on this wound until the medics get here,' he said. 'Your top won't do.' He sat back on his heels and peeled his t-shirt over his head.

Kate bit her lip. The moment was totally inappropriate, but she couldn't help watching as his tanned skin moved over muscles.

She frowned when she saw his tattoo, wondering what it meant, then shook herself, realising that he was talking to her as he folded the fabric into a thick square and held it to Steve's leg.

'Hold this right here,' he said and shifted so that Kate could take his place.

He turned at the sound of running feet and stood.

Emrah's second-in-command, flanked by four of his men, joined them at the intersection.

The men shook hands.

'It's good to see you, Ali.'

The Turk nodded towards the garage. 'Who do we have?'

'Yusuf, alive, chained to a homemade bomb,' said Finn. 'You might want to tread carefully – it could still go off. Two dead. Kaan escaped just before you got here. Where's Emrah?'

'He went after Kaan – apparently one of our men saw him leave the building.' Ali put his radio to his lips. 'We'll put out an alert on the airport and docks. I'll get military roadblocks on all the roads out of the city.'

Finn nodded. 'Good – hopefully that will flush him out.'

They turned at the sound of shouting.

One of Emrah's men slid to a halt next to them, his face pale in the evening light. 'Sir – we just found our comms specialist's body behind an industrial bin in the alley next to the garage. He's been stabbed sir.'

Ali frowned. 'Clothes?'

'Gone sir – stripped.'

Finn turned away and cursed. 'Kaan.'

Ali nodded. 'It would certainly seem so.' He brought the radio to his lips once more, then looked at it and changed his mind, tossing it to the floor.

'That makes our radio comms a problem.' He pulled out a mobile phone and dialled a number. 'I'll let Emrah know,' he said, and then turned away and began talking in rapid Turkish.

Kate turned her back on the conversation and carefully lifted the makeshift bandage from Steve's thigh. Blood soaked through the layers, and she shuffled closer to the wounded man.

'Steve?'

He opened his eyes and looked up at her, then lifted his hand off his leg.

Blood seeped between his fingers, and Kate noticed the wound bubbling with each heartbeat.

Steve reached out with his hand, and she took it in hers, and then she shifted on the ground so she could cradle his head in her lap. He squeezed her fingers.

'How bad is it?' she whispered.

'Hurts like hell.'

'Emrah's men are here. There's an ambulance on the way.'

He nodded. Loosening his grip on her, he reached into his jacket and drew out a piece of paper, before handing it to Kate.

She took it, and then frowned as she realised it was a photograph, creased around the corners, and depicting a good-looking couple in their thirties.

On the right of the picture, a lithe woman with long blonde hair tucked under a baseball cap grinned at the camera, her blue eyes sparkling against her tanned skin. On her left arm, the black outline of a tattoo traced across her skin, while a thin silver chain hung over her vest top.

Kate blinked, and looked again.

The tattoo.

Her eyes turned to the man in the picture. His face was turned towards the woman, his eyes only for her, the skin crinkled at the edges as he laughed with her.

Finn.

Kate swallowed hard.

His tattoo was the perfect mirror image of the woman's.

Kate turned and looked over her shoulder to where Finn now stood with Emrah's second-in-command, talking, pointing towards the building, and finalising the operation.

Her eyes travelled down to his bicep and the unfinished tattoo which poked out from under the sleeve of his t-shirt.

'Not unfinished,' she murmured. 'Half of one.'

She turned at a groan from Steve and noticed the blood from his wound was increasing, the man's face turning pale.

'Steve?'

His eyes flickered open. 'Hang onto the photograph. She meant a lot to us. Keep it safe, okay?'

'I will.' She grasped his hand tighter. 'But I'll give it back to you.'

A faint smile crossed his lips. 'Go and find out where that bloody ambulance is.'

She stood and ran towards Finn, who turned and frowned at the sound of her voice.

'I think Steve's in trouble.'

Finn pushed past her and grabbed hold of Steve's hand. 'Steve – hang in there. There's an ambulance on the way, you hear me?'

The other man groaned. 'I'm getting too old for this.'

Finn smiled, and Kate noticed the tears welling up in his eyes. She put her hand on his shoulder and slipped the battered photograph into her pocket.

The sound of sirens pierced the night air as the emergency vehicles drew closer.

'Go and meet them,' said Finn, pushing Kate away. 'Show them where to find us – hurry.'

Kate stood and ran across the intersection. Stepping out into the street, she closed her eyes and lifted her head towards the evening sky, taking a deep breath, her first real taste of freedom.

She exhaled, and then opened her eyes. The moon had risen fully and now bathed the buildings in a soft hue, softening the harsh lines of the stonework and leaving the surface cool to her touch.

Her head turned at the sound of the sirens reaching the end of the street, the lights from the emergency vehicles reflecting off the walls of the buildings as they drew closer. She waved her arms as they approached, drawing them to her. The vehicles slewed to a stop, two police cars followed by an ambulance, and the sirens fell silent.

Kate rushed to the police officer who stepped from the passenger seat of the first car, ignoring the man's reaction as he fumbled for his gun, still holstered.

'Help us!' said Kate. 'There's an injured man over here.' She tugged on the policeman's arm, pulling him with her. 'He needs a doctor – quickly!'

The policeman looked over his shoulder at his colleagues and nodded, then beckoned the ambulance personnel towards the small crowd of armed men. 'Wait here,' he told them, and then followed Kate up the street, his partner close behind.

As soon as the policemen saw Steve on the ground and the damage to his leg, they called back to the waiting medics.

The policeman pushed Finn out of the way and began tearing open Steve's jeans, exposing the wound. The medics pushed past and Kate turned away, unable to watch.

She tugged the photograph from her pocket, her thumb brushing against a spot of Steve's blood and streaking it across the image. She glanced over her shoulder at Finn, who was standing with his arms crossed and glaring at the emergency team who were now lifting Steve onto a stretcher and carefully wheeling him along the street to the waiting vehicle.

The first policeman turned to Finn and Ali and exchanged words. Kate couldn't hear what was said, but suspected it was the name of the hospital where they were taking the injured man. Finn nodded, and the policeman patted him once on the shoulder before turning and hurrying down the stairs after his colleagues.

Kate heard the sound of doors slamming, and then the sirens began to echo off the walls of the street as the ambulance drove away.

Finn was beside her before she had time to react. He snatched the photograph out of her fingers.

'Where did you get this?'

'Steve gave it to me. He asked me to look after it for him.'

Kate turned and began to walk towards the waiting car that Emrah's men had organised. She paused and looked over her shoulder. 'She's very pretty. I hope you were happy together.'

One of the policemen opened the door for her, and she climbed in.

'Please take me to my hotel now,' she said. She bowed her head as the car moved away and tears began to fall onto her cheeks.

Chapter 31

Kate rubbed the towel over her wet hair and hurried out of the bathroom.

After the police driver had dropped her off at the hotel, Kate had found fresh clothes laid out for her on her hotel bed. The driver had waited outside the door while she'd changed, and then took her old clothes to be passed onto the police forensics unit, after asking her to place them in a plastic bag.

Once he'd left, Kate had taken full advantage of the facilities, making liberal use of the complimentary shampoo and soap.

Slipping a t-shirt over her head, she stepped into new denim jeans and buttoned them up while walking through the spacious apartment.

Another impatient knock on the door hammered through the living area.

'Hang on – I'm coming.'

She threw the towel onto an armchair and ran her fingers through her hair, tucked her shirt into the waistband of her jeans, and padded barefoot towards the door.

'Who is it?'

'Me.'

She ripped the door open, pulling the price tag off the back of her jeans and throwing it into the wastepaper basket. She glared at the man standing in front of her.

'What do you want?'

Finn stood in the corridor, his hands in the pockets of his jeans. 'I wanted to explain.'

'There's nothing to explain,' said Kate. She pushed a strand of loose hair behind her ear.

'But I wanted to.'

She sighed. 'Finn – thank you for rescuing me. I'm sure Hart Enterprises will reward you for everything you've done, but I'm tired of hearing about bombs and any other sort of weapons. I understand that you probably have some issues to work through, but I'm not the one to help you with that.'

She began to close the door and jumped when his hand shot out and pushed against it.

'Wait.'

Her heart drummed in her chest. 'What?'

He pulled his other hand from his jeans and held it out to her. 'I wanted you to see these.'

She frowned, and slid the chain off the door, opening it fully. 'What are they?'

'Take them.'

She held out her hand and he tipped two metal cylinders into her palm. She looked up at him, confused.

'They're what Ian was meant to give to Kaan. That's what this was all about. In case Ian doesn't tell you.'

She sighed and took a step back. 'You'd better come in.'

He followed her through the door, closed it behind him, and then frowned when he saw her limping.

'Is your ankle still hurting?'

'It's fine. Have a seat.' She waved a hand towards the sofa, pulling out a chair from beneath the small dining table for herself. 'Please.'

He sat down awkwardly on the soft fabric seat and leaned forward, resting his arms across his knees.

Kate rolled the cylinders in her hand.

'What are they?'

'Some sort of part which goes into a rocket-propelled grenade,' said Finn. He shrugged. 'I don't know the specifics, but apparently Ian had just signed a deal with the Turkish military to develop these and provide them in batches over the next twelve months.'

'Legitimate?'

He nodded. 'That part was.'

She raised an eyebrow and waited for him to continue.

'Six months ago he was approached by a man calling himself Claude van Zant. Van Zant had apparently heard about the Turkish deal and wanted to buy the same parts. Ian agreed in principal, with a view to finalising the deal with van Zant when he arrived in Istanbul three weeks ago.'

Kate frowned. 'I don't know the name.'

'You won't. This is something Ian was pursuing without your knowledge. It's not the first time he's done this either – trying to do a deal outside of the business to avoid paying tax.'

'What happened? What went wrong?'

Finn stood and began pacing the room. 'When Steve and I arrived, we'd never heard of van Zant so we used our contacts to start running some checks.' He walked over to where she sat and ran his fingers over the metal cylinders in her hand. 'Van Zant didn't exist.'

'What do you mean?' Kate blinked and tried to ignore the shock which travelled through her skin at his touch.

'The man Ian who had agreed to sell these to was someone whose real name was Yusuf.'

Kate shuddered.

'He worked for someone called Kaan who's the self-appointed leader of a rebel group,' said Finn. 'He wants to overthrow the Turkish government and stop them from joining the European Union. Kaan is a terrorist. He wants to control the eastern part of the country for himself, and he'll use the current situation between the Kurdish rebels and the Turkish government to fuel his cause.'

'What did Ian do?' Kate whispered.

'Tried to pull out of the deal,' said Finn, taking his hand away. 'Except Kaan wouldn't let him – he was too close to getting a brand new state-of-the-art weapon which would put him on a level playing field with his sworn enemy – the Turkish military.'

'So he kidnapped me to get Ian to hand over the parts,' said Kate. 'Why didn't the Harts go to the police? Why get you and Steve involved?'

'Kaan told Ian that he'd kill you immediately if they went to the police.'

Kate put the cylinders down and walked over to the balcony window, the net curtains billowing in the breeze. She pushed a wisp of hair from her eyes and willed her mind to stop working overtime. She reminded herself that she was safe, that the terrorist was on the run, hiding from the authorities.

She looked back at Finn where he stood, his arms folded across his chest as he watched her.

'How is Steve?'

'Sore, but he'll be okay in a week or so,' said Finn smiling, and then his face grew serious. 'He's had worse.'

Kate bit her bottom lip and turned back towards the open window, not trusting herself to look at Finn.

With a few days' stubble across his face and his hair mussed up, his scent permeating through the room, she was all too aware of the effect he was having on her.

She closed her eyes. *It's just a reaction from the danger*, she reminded herself. *And the fact that a few hours ago, he walked into a building full of terrorists and rescued you.*

She opened her eyes and turned to him. 'Where's Cynthia?'

Finn looked down at the floor. 'I think it's called "helping the police with their enquiries",' he mumbled.

'What do you mean?'

Finn sighed. 'Cynthia thought you were the one Ian was having an affair with. It was Cynthia who told the terrorists about you to make Ian hand over the parts.'

Kate gasped. '*Cynthia* did this to me?'

Finn nodded. 'Once Ian had been exposed for selling the parts to Yusuf – or van Zant as they thought he was – Cynthia was going to take over the business and run it herself. Turns out the woman who Ian *had* been having an affair with was a prostitute –

used by Yusuf as a trap to capture you. Once they had mapped out your usual route to the boutique store where she insisted Ian buy her gifts from, the rest was easy.'

Kate turned, strode across the room, picked up the cushions from the sofa and threw them across the room, hitting a picture frame, the frustration burrowing out of her.

She'd been used – first by Ian, then by Cynthia – and all for their own selfish ideals of money and power.

She kicked over one of the stools next to the breakfast bar, and then swept a vase of flowers off its surface, sending the glassware and its contents crashing to the floor.

With a low growl, Finn strode across the room. He grabbed her by the shoulders and turned her towards him.

'Stop it, Kate. It's over. It's all over.'

Seizing her face between his hands, he traced his thumbs over her jaw line, his green eyes smouldering.

'Cynthia told me what happened to you as a kid. I'm so sorry I couldn't stop it happening again,' he said.

She struggled first, angry, then as his fingers began to smooth her hair, she gazed up at him, her breathing heavy. She gasped as he moved closer and bent down, his mouth only a fraction from hers.

'You drive me crazy,' he murmured, 'did I ever tell you that?'

His hands moved slightly as he drew her face to his, then he parted her lips with his tongue and tasted her.

She groaned as his mouth moved with hers, then melted into his grip as his hands moved down her neck, over her shoulders and began to stroke her breasts through her shirt. She felt her nipples turn hard, erect under his touch. A warm sensation began in her chest, worked its way down her stomach and flushed between her thighs.

He drew back, his breathing heavy. 'If we start this, I don't know if I'm going to be able to stop – are you okay with that?'

She nodded, mutely.

He groaned, and then pulled her close to him.

She could feel him now, the hardness of him against her stomach. She lifted her chin to meet his kiss, and whimpered as he began to gently nibble on her bottom lip.

She ran her tongue against his teeth, teasing, and then drew away with a gasp as he ran his hands over her still erect nipples.

She pulled away, and he frowned.

'What is it?'

'I want you,' she whispered. 'Right here, right now. I've never felt so safe.'

He pulled her to him, lifted her up and carried her across the room. He kicked open the door to the bedroom and deposited her on the bed.

The curtains danced in the breeze through the window, sunlight flickering across their faces as he began to pull at her shirt, tearing it free from her jeans.

'Let me,' she said, unbuttoning her shirt as he watched, his eyes never leaving her. When her shirt was undone, she tugged it down her arms then tossed it onto the floor. 'Your turn.'

He smiled, sat up and pulled his t-shirt over his head, then began to unbutton his jeans, lying on his back and thrusting his hips upwards. She moved closer as the buttons came undone and he freed himself.

'I would have thought it was too cold to go commando,' she smiled.

'I was in a rush.'

He kicked his jeans to one side, rolled over and pulled her to him. She groaned as his hands moved over her body, caressing the lean muscles under her skin, until his fingers reached her belt buckle.

'Wait,' he whispered, before loosening her jeans and pulling them down over her bottom. He rolled then, and she felt the soft fabric of the sheets on her skin. He straddled her, carefully lifted her towards him and loosened her bra. She gasped as her stomach brushed against the fullness of him, swollen and erect.

He pushed her back down to the sheets, and then lowered himself. 'I've wanted to do this to you since I first saw you,' he murmured. He ran his hand down the length of her body, his fingers rippling over her ribs until he found what he was seeking.

Her hips moved in response as his hand first cupped her mound, and then she gasped as he extended his fingers. Immediately the wetness consumed her.

'God you're perfect,' he said, lowering his mouth to her breasts, then slowly took one of her nipples between his lips and tugged.

She cried out, arching her back as his fingers began to rub, his tongue matching their rhythm.

Her breath came in small, desperate gasps, and he groaned, the vibration of his voice sending new sensations through her body. Her body began to shudder uncontrollably, and Finn raised his head, his liquid eyes watching her in the sunlight as she drew closer and closer to her climax, his fingers seeking it out, faster and faster until she could hold back no more.

She cried his name as she crested the wave of sensations which tore through her body, before she shuddered through her climax.

She lay, panting, until he gathered her up in his arms and lifted her.

'Don't think you're going to get all the fun,' he said huskily.

He rolled over, and then pulled her towards him until she could straddle him.

'Tell me that you want me,' she said.

His dark eyes flickered over her body. 'You have no idea how much I want you.' He cupped her breasts, sending shivers through her body once more.

She smiled and put her hands on his shoulders, and slowly edged down him.

His eyes closed and he groaned as she took him in.

His hands moved from her breasts, then down her body until he had her bottom in his grip, their breathing coming in short gasps as he reached his peak.

Suddenly, he was there. He thrust his hips up to meet hers, and she gasped at the depths he found within her. She cried out as her climax matched his, and gripped his shoulders, digging her fingers into his skin as his body shook beneath hers.

He shouted then, as he expelled everything within him, before falling back, panting, sweat pouring down his chest.

'Who was she?'
    'Hmm?'

'The girl in the photo.' Kate raised herself up onto her elbow and traced her finger over the fine hairs across Finn's chest. 'Who was she?'

Finn raised an eyebrow. 'How did you know she was dead?'

'Steve might have mentioned it.'

Kate rested her cheek on the pillow. 'She obviously meant a lot to you.'

Finn turned his head away from her.

She heard him exhale loudly, before he lifted his hand and rubbed the palm of it across his eyes.

'I can't talk about it,' he murmured. 'Not yet.'

'Finn – I know you're hurting, but I'd like to help you.'

'Please, Kate. Leave it alone.'

Kate flinched, and watched as he sat up and swung his legs over the edge of the bed.

Seconds passed, and then he stood and reached for his jeans. He pulled them on and turned to her.

'I can't talk about it,' he repeated and held up his hands. 'Don't ask me to, please.'

Kate's jaw dropped. 'I'm – I'm sorry. I just thought…'

'Don't, okay?' Finn sighed, and then checked his watch. 'I'm not going to discuss it now.' His voice was muffled as he pulled his t-shirt over his head, before he bent down and kissed her on the forehead. 'I'll see you later.'

'What?'

She swung the sheet away and followed him out to the living area, tying a bathrobe around her body.

Finn stood by the open door. 'I should probably get back to Hart's office.' He turned and began to walk away down the hallway.

Kate closed the door before Finn could hear her sob.

She turned to the room, her hand over her mouth and closed her eyes, tears streaking her cheeks.

After everything she'd been through, she'd hoped he'd show *something* other than a quick roll in the sheets if he had any feelings for her.

She opened her eyes and looked at the metal cylinders on the kitchen bench, then shook her head, crossed her arms over her breasts and hugged herself.

'Nice one, Kate,' she murmured. 'Got your hopes up again.'

Chapter 32

Kate thanked the taxi driver, got out of the car and walked into the entrance of the modern hospital building.

Pushing her way through the throng of people in the foyer, she approached the reception desk, got directions and took an elevator up to the sixth floor.

It wasn't hard to find Steve's room. Emrah had taken the liberty of placing two armed guards outside the door.

She showed them her European driving licence, assured them she wouldn't stay long and pushed the door open.

Steve's head turned at the sound of her approach, and he smiled.

Kate's hand flew to her mouth, and she choked back a sob.

The man's face looked grey, bruised, and a large swathe of bandages covered his leg.

'Don't start crying, lass,' he said. 'You're not exactly a pretty picture yourself.'

A laugh bubbled up, and Kate smiled. 'Thanks. Just what I needed to hear.'

She moved across the room and sat in the chair next to Steve, who reached over for the television remote and silenced it. An English premier league game played on in silence on the screen bolted to the opposite wall.

'How bad is it?' she asked.

'Hurts like hell,' he said. 'But it won't kill me.'

He pressed a button and the bed eased him upright.

Kate noticed he didn't bother to hide the pain which etched his face with the movement. She stood and carefully arranged the pillows behind his back to make him more comfortable.

'Where's Finn?' he said, once he'd settled back.

Kate sat down and looked at her hands. 'I don't know.'

Steve cocked an eyebrow and stayed silent.

Kate sighed. 'He was pretty pissed off about me having the photograph. And then,' she sniffed. 'I asked about the girl in the picture, and he walked out on me.'

'Ah. I see.'

'You'll have to get it back from him. He took it from me.'

Steve shrugged. 'No need – it was his anyway.'

'Excuse me?'

'I took it from him three years ago. He'd walk around all day moping over it. I figured the only way to kick-start his recovery was to take it from him. I told him he could have it back when he sorted himself out.'

'Oh.' She watched the football game in silence for a moment, and then turned back to him.

'What happened?'

Steve exhaled a long sigh. 'It's about time someone told you – although it should have been Finn,' he said. 'I really thought he'd give you a chance.' He cleared his throat.

Kate thought he was almost psyching himself up to tell her, so she waited, wanting to know, but scared that she might not like the answer.

'The girl in the photograph? She was my daughter,' he said.

Kate looked sharply at him.

'Yeah, I know – I should've told you before,' he said. 'But there's never an easy time, or a better way, is there?'

He didn't wait for an answer, and Kate sensed that he'd been waiting a long time to tell someone what had happened three years ago, so she kept quiet and listened while Steve told her how his daughter, Claire, had been dating Finn for over a year.

The couple had been infatuated with each other, hence the matching tattoos. They'd met eighteen months before a function organised by the British Trade Commission in Miami where she'd undertaken a new role as a media liaison officer.

Finn had been assigned to the function by his FBI bosses to provide protection to a Mexican dignitary who had been openly threatened the previous week by a drug cartel back home.

Claire had followed a handful of dignitaries to a back room where a new tri-partisan oil agreement was to be signed by all parties, when the room was breached by armed gunmen. She and the Mexican delegate were forcibly taken while a pitched battle at the venue resulted in four dead bodyguards, including two of Finn's men, and two very shaken British and American signatories.

Finn had led the hostage rescue team which had been tasked with retrieving Claire and the Mexican politician when the gunmen's hideout had been discovered hours later. Finn was only allowed to lead the team because he was nearer, rather than the FBI having to wait for another team to get there.

His superiors didn't want him involved because of the personal connection, but he left them with no choice. He was adamant.

Deemed a rescue and retrieve mission because it was highly unlikely Claire or the dignitary would be released after the shooting of the bodyguards, Finn and his team were given little time to plan their subsequent counter-attack, especially after both the British and American governments stoked the kidnappers' anger by publicly refusing to pay a ransom to a terrorist organisation.

The rescue went wrong – when Finn's team broke into the building, all hell broke loose with the bad guys fighting back. Steve's daughter panicked during the fire fight, and instead of keeping her head down as she'd been trained, she tried to run.

She was shot in the crossfire with two of the guys from Finn's team. It was still unknown whether an FBI agent shot her or one of the Mexican drug dealers.

When Finn started heading into a downward spiral, it was Steve who had approached his superiors and suggested Finn go and work for him at his hostage survival training business in the UK, because it would help turn something negative into a positive – to train others what not to do if caught in that situation.

Finn was honourably discharged from the FBI and went with Steve back to the north of England, where he'd been for the past three years.

'And then you walked through the door,' Steve smiled. 'That was the first time I'd seen a spark of life in Finn since that mission.'

Kate got up from her chair and walked across the room to the window.

Below, the mid-morning traffic threw a smog haze across the city, the noise muffled by the thick glass separating her from the world outside. Her knuckles whitened as she gripped the sill, and she leaned forward until her forehead rested against the cool glass.

'He's not a bad person,' said Steve. 'Being an asshole is his way of coping.'

Kate smiled and turned back to him, leaned against the window sill, and crossed her arms.

'What are you saying?'

Steve shrugged his right shoulder. 'That you could do worse.'

Kate spluttered a laugh. 'Oh I have, that's for sure.' She frowned. 'It must've been so hard for you.'

He nodded. 'It was. But my grief turned into concern for Finn. Okay, Claire died, and I wish to hell and back she was here now, but she's not. There was no sense watching another human being dig himself into an early grave because of it.'

He moved, and Kate saw the pain in his face. She walked quickly to his side and helped him lower the bed, until he nodded and she rearranged his pillows once more.

'How's that?'

'Eh, it'll do. I daren't take any morphine – I'm scared I'll get addicted.'

She frowned.

'Seen it happen,' he said. 'Guys take longer to get over that stuff than the actual injury. I'd rather feel myself heal.'

Kate smiled and sat down once more.

'What am I going to do, Steve?' she asked, looking at her hands.

'Give him a chance,' he said. 'Yeah, sure, he's a pain in the backside most of the time – but there's a heart of gold there. He'd do anything for you, you know.'

'Mmm. I'm not too sure about that at the moment.' She sighed, and then turned at a knock on the door.

Ali, Emrah's second-in-command, walked into the room and seemed unsurprised to see her.

'Miss Foster, I hope you're recovering from your ordeal?'

'Yes, thank you.'

He turned to Steve. 'Feel up to answering some preliminary questions?'

'Sure.'

Kate stood. 'I should let you two talk.'

'Thanks for coming by.'

She leaned over and kissed Steve's cheek. 'Stay out of trouble. I'll pop by in the next few days – see how you're doing.'

She shook Ali's hand as she left the room, and then nodded to the guards outside the door, and walked slowly along the corridor towards the exit, wondering how on earth she was going to break down the wall Finn had built around himself.

Chapter 33

Kate pushed the door to her hotel room open and heard something crackle under its weight.

She frowned, closed it, and then bent down and picked up the piece of paper which had been pushed underneath.

She eased out the creases, then unfolded it and read the note which had been scrawled along the top.

Will be back later. Need to explain. Finn.

She sighed. 'You sure do.'

She walked across to the balcony. Pulling the glass door open, she breathed in the fragrant air and listened to the sound of the traffic in the street below, the road bursting with life – car horns, music, and people shouting to each other.

She wondered if she'd ever be able to mend Finn's heart. Her mind wandered to the unfinished tattoo on his arm. She'd heard of people wearing their heart on their sleeve, but never a broken one – not so that it remained a permanent reminder of the pain.

She walked across the open-plan room into the kitchen, switched on the lights and poured herself a glass of red which a member of the hotel staff had arranged for her. She sighed, took a sip and wondered if her life would ever be the same again.

She spun at a knock on the door and hurried towards it, ripping it open.

'Finn!'

She had no time to scream as Kaan pushed himself into the room, covered her mouth with an iron grip, his fingers squeezing hard, and slammed the door behind him.

They stared at each other, both breathing heavily.

Kate struggled to free herself, but Kaan's strength overpowered her in seconds.

He spun her round until she was pressed up against his chest, his mouth against her ear.

'Is he here?' he hissed.

She felt his chin knock the back of her head as he twisted around, searching the apartment, then gasped as his arm snaked around her and grabbed her breast. 'Is he *here*?'

She squealed with the pain, and then shook her head.

Kaan spun her round to face him.

She opened her mouth to scream, but his hand shot to her throat and began to squeeze.

'Where are the cylinders?'

Kate's head shot back as he shook her, and she closed her eyes, refusing to look towards the kitchen bench, where the two bomb parts lay side by side, gleaming under the artificial lighting.

'Where are they?' Kaan shouted.

'I don't know!' Kate gasped. 'Finn took them.'

Kaan's grip eased off her throat, and he began to look round the room. He raised his head and sniffed the air before his gaze fell to her once more. 'When did he leave, bitch?'

Kate's skin prickled as he stepped away from her, his fingers caressing her throat. She tried to slow her breathing, sure that he could feel her pulse hammering in her neck.

Kaan's face turned to hers, a malevolent gleam in his eyes.

'Did I tell you what I do to liars?' he asked, tracing his fingers down her cheek.

Kate whimpered. 'Please – please don't hurt me.'

Kaan chuckled. 'Oh, I'm going to do a lot more than hurt you, Miss Foster. By the time I'm finished with you, no other man will want you.'

Kate lashed out with her foot, hitting the man in the shins.

He cried out, loosening his grip on her.

She pulled away, and then ran for the kitchen. Reaching the bench, she swept up one of the metal cylinders into her hand and turned.

In time to meet Kaan face to face, the man's fury etched in his eyes.

'You bitch,' he hissed and lunged for her.

The door to the apartment exploded inwards, a metal chair tearing through the wooden fabric.

Closely followed by Finn.

He pushed his shoulder into the broken pieces of the door, the panelling splintering under his weight, and stumbled into the room.

'Get your hands off her, Emrah, you bastard,' he snarled.

Kaan grinned. 'You finally worked it out, Mr Scott.'

Finn edged closer, watching the other man carefully. 'It always seemed to me that Kaan was a step ahead of us every time,' he said. 'I wasn't sure, Emrah, Kaan – whoever you are – until you disappeared after we rescued Kate.' He moved slowly forwards. 'But then I realised you wouldn't leave without the bomb parts so you could try again.'

Kate ducked out of Kaan's reach, grabbed the second cylinder, and rushed to the other side of the kitchen, keeping the counter between herself and Kaan.

Kaan leaned over and pulled a knife from the collection on the kitchen counter.

Kate scooted backwards until she was out of his reach and watched as he advanced towards Finn, waving the knife.

'You should have stayed away,' he said. 'We were nearly finished.'

Finn shook his head, his palms up, his eyes tracking the path of the knife as it slashed the air in front of him. 'Looks like I got here just in time.'

He leapt backwards as Kaan lurched towards him, the knife missing his chest by a fraction of a second. He spun to face the man, and Kate saw him glance at her briefly before he concentrated on the weapon once more.

She pulled herself to her feet and cast her eyes around the small kitchen, looking for something – anything – which could help Finn.

Kaan was circling now, getting closer while Finn ducked and dodged the blade.

Kate could see the expression on Finn's face as he used his peripheral vision to scan the room around him.

He stepped back, putting more distance between himself and Kaan, then bent down to the coffee table, picked up the remote control for the television and threw it hard at Kaan's face.

Kaan laughed and ducked, the remote striking his shoulder before falling to the floor.

Kate gasped as Finn backed up against the sofa, cornered. He looked behind him, and then leapt onto the cushioned seat, using the momentum to bounce over the back of the furniture. He turned his head left and right, searching for a weapon of his own, then began to pull books from the shelf against the wall, throwing them at Kaan.

The other man raised his arm against the onslaught, protecting his face while waving the blade and moving closer, gradually driving Finn from behind the sofa and back into the open space of the living area.

As the men circled each other, Kate reached up and pulled a frying pan off a hook on the wall, trying to keep as quiet as possible. Finn caught her eye, then began turning so that Kaan's back was to her. She kicked off her shoes and began to silently pad towards the man's back.

'Just give it up, Kaan,' panted Finn, 'The police will be here any minute. It'll go a lot better for you if you go quietly.'

Kaan laughed, a guttural sound which filled the air. 'So that you can be a hero? I don't think so,' he said. 'You will die here today. And while your life is bleeding out of you, you will watch what I do to your woman.'

He raised the knife and charged at Finn, who stepped backwards and tripped over the coffee table, falling to the floor.

Kaan swept down to the floor, advancing towards him as Finn pushed himself backwards, his eyes watching the path of the blade as it swung closer.

'You bastard!'

Kate rushed forwards, intending to beat Kaan across his head with the frying pan as hard as she could.

He turned round, fending off her attack and slashing out with the knife.

She screamed as the blade sliced through the sleeve of her blouse and nicked her skin, and dropped the pan in surprise. Kaan lurched forwards to grab her, and she turned and ran, putting the dining table between herself and the man.

Kate's eyes widened as Kaan advanced on her, then a movement from behind caught his attention and he spun round.

Finn groaned, and Kaan rushed towards him, the knife raised.

Finn scrambled to his feet and pulled a cushion from the sofa towards him. He lifted it into the air above his head as Kaan thrashed the knife down, the blade tearing through the fabric.

Finn flicked the cushion out of Kaan's reach, the knife still embedded between the material, and then threw it across the room. He turned back to the Turk, eyes blazing, waving him forward.

'Now we're even,' he said.

Kaan charged at him, grabbing him round his waist and powered him backwards across the carpeted floor towards the open balcony window.

Kate screamed out a warning to Finn, who grabbed a vase from a shelf as he staggered past it, struggling under the other man's weight to keep his balance, and brought the ornament crashing down across the man's back.

His grip on Finn loosened. Kate cried out as he stepped round the bigger man and wrapped his forearm across Finn's throat.

Finn's hands flew to Kaan's arms as he tried to weaken the other man's grip, his breathing harsh and desperate.

As they stumbled backwards past the writing bureau, Finn slid the hotel's leather-bound welcome pack towards him with his fingertips, then grabbed it, and began to beat it around Kaan's face.

Kate stood and slowly advanced towards the two men as they backed towards the open door and the narrow balcony beyond, willing Finn to wrench himself out of Kaan's grip. She caught Finn's eyes as he glared at her.

He had stopped trying to pry Kaan's fingers from his throat and was waving his hand in her direction, his finger jabbing the air.

She shook her head, frowned, and then watched as he repeated the action, the anger in his face terrifying her.

She looked behind, and realising what he was pointing at, rushed across the room to the kitchen bench, and picked up the aerosol can.

Kaan cried out as Finn suddenly jerked his head backwards, breaking Kaan's nose. Stunned, the terrorist released the bigger man, his hands covering his bloodied face.

'Finn!'

Kate threw the can of pepper spray to him.

He caught it, spun round and with both hands shoved Kaan away from him, then pressed the nozzle on the aerosol.

Kaan screeched, his hands rubbing at his eyes, and staggered backwards over the threshold, his arms flailing as he tried to regain his balance. He tripped, stumbled across the balcony, his hips hitting the cast iron railing.

Too late, Kate realised what was going to happen and turned her head, closing her eyes.

She couldn't avoid hearing the scream of terror from the man as his body hit the low railing before he catapulted into the night air, his screams cut short seconds later.

Chapter 34

Finn thanked Ali, assured him they would be at his office the next day for more interviews, and closed the door.

Kate stood in the middle of the room, her arms hugged to her sides to stop her hands from trembling.

'Sit down,' said Finn, pointing to one of the armchairs. 'I need to clean up.'

Kate lowered herself into the plush comfort of the suede material and drew her knees up to her chest.

Finn walked across to the small refrigerator in the kitchen, opened the door and pulled out two bottles of beer. He twisted the caps off, threw them in the sink then walked back to Kate and handed her one of the beers before clinking the bottle against his own.

'They don't seem to provide complimentary icepacks,' he said with a wry smile and held the cold bottle to his forehead.

Kate looked at the purple bruise beginning to form on his face and tried not to let him see her hands shaking as she took a sip of the beer. She put the bottle down on the coffee table next to the armchair and turned her head, wiping her eyes.

Finn crouched down next to her. A trickle of blood ran from a cut above his eye. He palmed it away distractedly, his fingers scabbed from the blows he'd landed on Kaan.

'I'm going to take a shower, get some of these cuts sorted out, okay?'

Kate nodded, her eyes scanning the room.

Finn followed her gaze. 'He's gone, Kate. Dead,' he said. 'Never coming back.'

A shaky sigh escaped her lips.

He stood and put a hand on her shoulder. 'Don't answer the door to anyone. I won't be long, okay?'

She nodded, and then watched as he moved across the room and then pushed the bathroom door shut behind him.

The sound of water hitting the tiles reached her ears, and she uncurled her legs, then stood and wandered across to the window. She felt awkward in Finn's hotel room, on edge.

The room was identical to hers, except that any trace of Finn's presence had been restricted to the small dining table near the window. On it, his notes from the past few days were strewn across the glass surface.

Kate palmed through them, observing his neat handwriting, the block capitals interspersed with arrows, sketches and question marks.

She paused as she uncovered the photograph which he'd taken from her. She glanced over her shoulder towards the bathroom door, and then picked it up.

The blood stain had been carefully removed, the corners pressed flat, as if it had been held recently.

'It's just your imagination,' she murmured, tucking it back under the notepaper.

Her mind replayed Kaan's attack and what would have happened to her if Finn hadn't returned when he had.

She frowned. Why had he come back? Had he seen Kaan?

She looked over her shoulder at the closed bathroom door.

Or had he come back for her, like he'd said in his note?

Her heartbeat rising, she stepped across the carpet to the bathroom door and leaned her head against it. Beyond, she could hear Finn under the water, and imagined the droplets flowing over his body.

A shiver of desire travelled down her spine, and then she jumped back as the door moved inwards under her weight.

Steam escaped into the living area, the creaking extractor fan a poor match for the temperature in the small bathroom. Beyond the steamed up shower door, Kate saw Finn standing with his back to her, his palms against the tiled wall as he let the jets of water cascade over his head.

She moved closer, her heart hammering, her mind screaming at her to walk away, to turn and go before he broke her heart like the others before him.

She ignored the doubts clouding her mind, remembering his touch on her skin. Slipping out of her jeans, she unbuttoned her blouse and let it fall to the floor. She took a deep breath and opened the door to the cubicle.

Finn's eyes blazed when he saw her, his initial look of surprise turning to lust in an instant.

Kate bit her bottom lip, suddenly unsure of herself as the steam escaped and swirled over her skin. She gazed at Finn's body as he turned towards her, and then blushed as she looked up and met his eyes.

He ran his fingers through his hair to slick it back off of his face, and then held out his hand.

'Come here,' he said. 'The water's perfect.'

She stepped towards him, into his arms, the heat from his body enveloping her. She closed her eyes and groaned as he tipped her head gently backwards, then began kissing her throat, her neck, down to her collarbone, then raised his head.

'I thought I'd lost you,' he murmured, his palm cupping her cheek.

She shook her head, felt tears pricking her eyes. 'You didn't lose me, Finn – you rescued me, remember?'

He smiled, reached around and undid her bra, letting it fall to the floor.

She saw the hunger in his eyes as he pulled her closer, slipped his fingers under the lace of her panties and slid them down her thighs.

'I don't think you're going to need these.'

Kate groaned as he pushed her against the tiled wall of the shower cubicle. She wrapped her arms around his neck and raised her lips to his, tasting him, nibbling at his tongue as it sought out her warmth.

She closed her eyes and moaned as his lips worked their way south, and cried out as he took each nipple in turn, caressing her breasts while the water pounded against their soaked bodies.

She felt his hand cup her jaw, and opened her eyes to meet his gaze.

'I'm not letting you out of my sight ever again,' he murmured. 'You okay with that?'

She nodded, running her fingers over his chest, feeling him shiver with desire under her touch. She worked her hands down his body until she could grasp the whole of him, pulling him closer until she could feel the firmness against her stomach.

His groan resounded off the tiles, and she felt him stagger slightly, before he gently pushed her back, then slid his hands under her thighs and lifted her to him.

As their bodies began to move, Kate closed her eyes and let the water stream over her face.

'Steve told me about his daughter,' said Kate. 'I'm so sorry, Finn.'

She heard him move across the sheets, and then sigh, his breath moving a stray hair over her face.

He gently brushed it away, and Kate closed her eyes, waiting for the explosion.

'And I'm sorry,' he said.

She opened her eyes and lifted her head to look at him.

He smiled. 'I'm sorry I was an asshole earlier.'

Her lips met his. 'You're forgiven. It must be incredibly hard to talk about.'

He nodded. 'I should try practicing once in a while.' He shifted his weight and pulled her closer. 'Especially when someone I care about asks me.'

Kate rested her cheek on his chest, saying nothing, soaking up his scent, his touch.

'I think Cynthia's truly remorseful about what she did to you,' Finn said. 'She's going to regret it for the rest of her life.'

'And what do you think?'

He pulled her down towards him.

'I think you're going to be okay.'

Chapter 35

Northumbria
Three months later

Kate lowered the binoculars from her eyes and squinted in the bright sunshine.

'Well, I can't see him.'

'Over there. To the left of the tree line. Follow it until you see a flash of white.'

She frowned and looked again. 'Got him.'

'Easy mistake to make. He can't resist looking for us, when he should be keeping his head down instead.'

Kate turned to Finn and smiled. 'Go get 'em.'

He grinned, reached out and tipped her chin towards him, before kissing her tenderly. 'I'll be back in time for lunch.'

She laughed and pushed him away. 'Just remember to play nice, okay?'

He waved to her over his shoulder, and then got into the four wheel drive next to Steve, and the vehicle bounced away down the hillside.

She smiled, and decided to watch the take-down, even though she knew the men's routine almost as well as they did.

The four wheel drive reached the bottom of the hill, then turned into the field and raced across to the line of birch and oak trees which formed a natural boundary between the fallow land and a river.

A second four wheel drive powered across the opposite end of the field towards the trees, while a small boat chugged along the river.

Kate smiled. It was cruel, but Finn and Steve had deliberately led the executives to believe that only two men would be hunting them. Instead, they'd decided to make the experience as realistic as possible, knowing the men would learn valuable lessons from it.

The executives they were hunting had booked onto the course to prepare for a trip they were planning to central Africa to raise money for a charity. At the charity's insistence, the course had to be undertaken as part of the volunteers' preparation before entering the country.

Kate raised the binoculars to her eyes. Fascinated, she watched the three men make the choices that would define how Finn and Steve would approach each of their 'interrogations'.

The first burst out of the undergrowth with his hands in the air, clearly tired of the whole process. A smile stole across Kate's lips. The man had already marked himself out to Finn and Steve after the classroom session the previous day, where he'd slouched in his seat, an arm slung across the back of it and a look of disinterest across his face.

She shook her head. She knew the men would frighten the executive into trying harder not to get caught the second time around.

The other two executives quickly disappeared amongst the trees, but forgot about the river. Within minutes, the boat was alongside them, the man in it crouched and ready with a rifle aimed at one of them. Each man put his hands in the air and fell to their knees as the second four wheel drive emptied its passengers and four armed men encircled the remaining executives.

She lowered the binoculars and made her way back to her vehicle, then drove down the track towards the farmhouse. She avoided the part of the building where the mock interrogations took place. It still chilled her that she'd been so close to losing her life three months ago.

Instead, she made her way through the farmhouse, past the kitchen where caterers were busy finalising the lunch which would be set out in a few hours, and entered the office.

Steve had been adamant about Finn taking over the company and, after a lot of persuasion, managed to convince him it was the right thing to do.

In turn, Finn had pointed out that Kate no longer had a job – or an employer – and if the business was going to build on its success, it needed a decent business development manager to oversee it.

In the end, the three of them had agreed that Steve would take a back seat on the day-to-day running of the business, while Finn ran the operations side and Kate managed the sales.

Between them, they'd quickly built up an impressive client list and were now in a position where the diary was booked up months in advance by journalists, aid workers, and volunteer organisations.

Kate sank into the leather bound chair behind her desk and began sifting through the morning's paperwork. Two weeks ago, she'd admitted defeat and had taken on a part-time administrator to help her, but force of habit meant that she still kept a keen eye on the office administration.

The back door to the farmhouse slammed shut and muffled shouts echoed down the flagstone passageway as, one by one, the 'hostages' were brought in and taken into individual rooms.

Kate leaned over and switched on her favourite music playlist, turned the volume up and went back to work, tapping her foot to the rock music which bled from the speakers.

She glanced at her watch. The first session was designed to run for an hour, in order to monitor the executives for any health problems which might surface during the longer mock interrogations.

Kate's heart beat rapidly, and she forced herself to concentrate on the task in hand, rather than thinking about what the men would be going through, her memories still too raw.

She shook her head. Finn had told her that her experience would make her an ideal manager for the business, and she had agreed at the time. She told herself that it would get better, but for now, she coped as best she could and took each day one at a time.

The hour passed quickly, and by the time Kate had emailed the last person on her 'to do' list, the sound of laughter and catcalling reached her office.

She switched off the computer, wandered past the kitchen to make sure the caterers were ready and then made her way through to the dining room.

'Ah, there she is,' said Finn and waved her over to the group.

'How did it go?'

'We're just waiting for one more to join us,' he said. 'He's in with Steve.'

Kate noticed the wicked smile on his face and guessed who the latecomer was. 'I see,' she said, and then turned at the sound of one of the doors in the passageway opening.

The languid executive who had sat in the classroom the day before had disappeared. In his place, a pale, slightly sickly looking man emerged from the interrogation experience.

Steve followed him, and slapped him on the shoulder as they walked into the dining room.

'I hope you've got a good appetite, Matthew,' he said, winking theatrically at the rest of the room. 'Kate's been slaving all morning in the kitchen just for you.'

Stifled laughter filled the split-second silence which followed his remark, and Kate noticed that the executive managed to look a little sheepish as he joined his colleagues and ran his hand through his hair.

'That was so much harder than I thought,' he mumbled, then had the graciousness to join in the laughter which followed.

Kate walked up to him and handed him a bottle of water. 'Drink this slowly at first,' she instructed. 'Just in case, okay?'

The man nodded, and then turned back to his colleagues.

Kate turned to see Finn smiling at her and walked over to join him, sitting next to him and uncapping her own bottle of water.

'And how are you doing?'

Finn smiled and lifted the white padding from his bicep.

Kate leaned across and pulled it away with her finger, the black ink of the completed tattoo gleaming under the new skin.

She glanced up at Finn and smiled. 'It's healing well.'

'Mmm. The guy it's painted on isn't doing too badly either.'

Kate grinned, then stood and recapped the bottle of water and set it to one side.

'Okay folks, let's get back into it. We've got a lot to cover in a short space of time today. One hour for a lunchbreak, and then we'll let you know what we've got in store for you this afternoon.'

The executives began to settle into their seats. One of them leaned forward and looked down the length of the dining table towards Finn and Kate.

'What happens if we're kidnapped, and then they move us?' he asked.

Kate looked across to Finn, who nodded at her.

Kate smiled at him, and then turned back to the class.

'Whatever it takes – they'll find you.'

From the Author

Thanks for purchasing and reading *Before Nightfall* - I hope you enjoyed it. A lot of people don't realise that the best way to help an author is to write a review – if you did enjoy this story, please return to the site you bought it from and leave a few words.

I love hearing from readers and other authors alike, so if you'd like to stay in touch and be the first to find out about forthcoming novels, why not drop by and visit me at:

www.rachelamphlett.com

Facebook: Rachel Amphlett - Author

Twitter: @RachelAmphlett

You can also join my mailing list to receive free extracts from my other novels by completing the form on my website:
http://www.rachelamphlett.com/contact.html

I look forward to hearing from you.

Acknowledgements

Every writer needs a tribe, and I'm no different.

Thanks to the following people for their feedback and support during the writing process for *Before Nightfall*: Christine Edwards, John and Marilyn Miles, Jackie Parry, Richard Smith, and Donna Joy Usher.

To Sally Collings, Derek Murphy and Danielle Rose – your professionalism and advice brought this novel to life. I look forward to working with you again soon.

To my family and friends – thanks for allowing me to lock myself away for hours on end doing what I love. I apologise if I haven't returned your phone call or emails. I am a terrible friend once a story gets hold of me, so I look forward to catching up soon.

Finally, to everyone who's been following me on Twitter, Facebook and Goodreads, etc since my writing journey began – your reviews and messages of support always seem to find me when I most need them, so thank you. It means a lot to know you enjoy reading my novels as much as I enjoy writing them.

Until next time,

Rachel Amphlett – Brisbane, 2014

White Gold

A Dan Taylor novel

When Sarah Edgewater's ex-husband is murdered by a radical organisation hell-bent on protecting their assets, she turns to Dan Taylor – geologist, ex-soldier, and lost cause.

Together, they must unravel the research notes that Sarah's ex-husband left behind to locate an explosive device which is circumnavigating the globe towards London – and time is running out.

In a fast-paced ecological thriller which spans the globe, from London to Brisbane and back via the Arctic Circle, Dan and Sarah aren't just chasing the truth – they're chasing a bomb which, if detonated, will change the future of alternative energy research and the centre of England's capital forever.

eBook ISBN: 978-0-646-55814-1

Paperback ISBN: 978-0-646-57340-3

Under Fire

A Dan Taylor novel

An explosion rocks a Qatari natural gas facility… a luxury cruise liner capsizes in the Mediterranean… and someone has stolen a submarine…

Are the events connected?

Dan Taylor doesn't believe in coincidences – all he has to do is convince his superiors they are next in the terrorists' line of fire.

As Britain enters its worst winter on record, Dan must elude capture to ensure the country's energy resources are protected. At all costs.

In an action-packed adventure, from the Middle East through the Mediterranean to London, Dan and his team are on a quest which will test every choice he makes. Assisted by the exotic Antonia Almasi, Dan realises he faces an adversary far greater than he ever imagined.

And not everyone is going to survive.

eBook ISBN: 978-0-992-26851-0

Paperback ISBN: 978-0-992-26850-3